The Lending Library

C. L. Kraemer

Published by Rogue Phoenix Press, LLP
Copyright © 2020

ISBN: 978-1-62420-537-8

Cover Art: Designs by Ms. G

Prologue

Follow the highway that hugs the shoreline of the river about fifteen miles into the dense forest. A covered bridge spanning the water appears on the right side. Turn your vehicle slowly onto the creaky, wooden single lane passage and after holding your breath and praying the bridge holds your vehicle, follow the narrow lane for three miles. The transport through a rainbow of greenery is unlike any other spot on this planet. Towering pines reach their evergreen arms to the sky creating a canopy that provides a cool shelter for the creatures of the forest. As the fading blue of the overhead sky begins to morph into inky darkness, the road wends itself past a slatted building tucked into a crook within the wooded landscape. The clapboard siding could do with a coat of paint and visitors must wonder if the shaky building will stand another year in this coveted haven. Much of the outside bears the weathered scars left by years of rain and a slight green sheen to the sides indicate the moss which cushions the foot on the forest floor has decided to overtake the structure thus returning the elements back to their beginning. The one inconsistent in this picture is the sturdy, new porch hosting miniscule tables and chairs.

A sign out front bears white, chipped letters of explanation:
The Lending Library--open 24 hours. Welcome.

Linda Brown moved to these woods so long ago she'd forgotten the actual date. She hated the isolation at first, but after spending ten years being miserable, she realized she had a choice to make--move or learn to adjust. She adjusted.

It was after she'd adjusted to her situation she discovered mail order catalogs and book clubs. When her husband Donald passed away, she gave away all the earthly things he had felt so important and built shelves in every room except the kitchen to store her books and create her library. She moved her small bed into the old pantry adding a small window so she might see the "little people" when they came to visit her before she fell asleep.

Friends from her socializing days stopped visiting. People in town began calling her the Witch of the Woods and quit passing by the house. Linda didn't care. She had her library and the wee ones.

Chapter One

Ailidh wobbled precariously on her high heels.

Kayne smirked. "Having problems, dear?"

"Shut up!" she snapped. "I need to practice this until I get it right. We don't really have many options left open to us, Kayne. You had better practice, too."

He stopped and steadied himself on the railing of the porch. He wriggled his feet out of the closed leather shoes that encased them.

"I don't know why you insist we wear these ridiculous articles of clothing. This long-sleeved shirt cuts off the circulation to my hands not to mention the lack of space for my wings and these long pants chap my legs.

"Worst of all, are these horrendous leather shoes. They pinch and make my feet swell. Why do we have to go through all of this? I don't understand." Kayne grumbled.

Ailidh sighed and slowly, *patiently* explained to him, once again, why they were practicing.

"Remember last Wednesday when Keegan and Connal lost their dwelling? The sound of their tree crashing to the ground was deafening. The Others are moving out more and more. We will lose our home if we don't act first. Now, put your shoes back on and walk for just five more minutes."

Kayne wrestled his shirt off and threw it to the porch's deck. He pulled the long pants off his body and left them in a heap next to the shirt. Bending forward, he touched his toes gingerly as he gradually unfurled his lacey wings. Slowly, he pulled himself to an upright position. Shoulders back, wings completely expanded, he lifted his 18-inch form to its full height and looked at Ailidh defiantly.

"I don't need to fit into the Others' world. They need to adjust themselves to my world and leave us alone."

Ailidh, teetering, grabbed the lower railing of the porch and shook her head.

"Kayne, most of the Others don't even know we exist. How can they adjust to something they don't even believe?"

"They adjust to animals, don't they?"

"The animals chose to be seen. We did not. Remember? Our great, great grandfathers took a vote and decided we would endanger ourselves more if we continued to be visible to the Others. At that time, they didn't have all the machinery they have now. They moved into our lands at a slower pace. Now, put on the clothes and try to adjust."

"No." Kayne kicked at the clothing on the porch. "I'm going to get a magazine and a cup of coffee. You can stand here and practice day and night for all I care."

He turned on his heels and lifted himself off the ground with his delicate appendages. He lazily winged his way into the open window of the building marked *Lending Library*.

Hovering until he landed on the balls of his feet, he folded the wings tight to his torso and walked to the corner of the building signed Coffee Shop. He sat in a small chair snugged close to the matching table. Sliding the Newsweek someone had tossed on the table toward him, he flipped through the pages. Minimized for easier handling, the magazine was still large enough to require both of his hands to turn the pages. A diminutive nymph in a waitress uniform with a "Chrissy" nametag took his order for a latte. Ten minutes later, she returned with the steaming liquid in a cup.

"Thanks, Chrissy." Kayne picked up the cup carefully and took a sip.

"No problem, Kayne," she had a surprisingly deep voice for a nymph. "Where's Ailidh?"

Kayne jerked a thumb over his shoulder toward the front porch.

4

"Practicing," he grunted.

"Oh," Chrissy mopped the table next to Kayne's with a wet rag then flew daintily to the kitchen with the dirty cups and saucers she'd picked up. One of the resident dryads of the valley, Chrissy was living in the tree behind the Lending Library. Her home across the meadow had been one of the first destroyed.

Ailidh is right. Kayne frowned at the silent admission. The Others were invading his world with frightening, swift, uncaring swaths into the forestlands. Soon there wouldn't be an Ancient tree left. While, at a glance, their movements seemed random, even careless, Kayne had noted a pattern, albeit haphazard, to their actions. Months earlier he'd watched from a safe distance as the huge screeching yellow machines ripped up his ancient wood friends and squashed their bodies beneath armored tracks. He could never be sure whether the squealing had been the old trees or the vicious yellow machines. After the first occasion of watching as they destroyed a sea of Ancients, Kayne had left on shaky wings and flown home. Ailidh was furious at him, thinking he'd been with his friends drinking honeysuckle wine. He couldn't stop throwing up long enough to tell her what he'd seen.

When the thunder and growl of the angry yellow tree destroyers rumbled over their living room ceiling several months later, Kayne sat Ailidh down and explained what had happened that fateful night.

He took her soft, dainty hand in his and looked into her sparkling moss green eyes.

"We must be prepared to move from our home."

Ailidh's exquisite wings trembled. "Why?"

The earth near the entrance to their home groaned and bits of dirt drizzled from around the doorway.

Kayne pointed up. "That--that--monster will reach into our home and pluck us up with no regard whatsoever. I've seen it rip out the Ancient trees in the glen over by Drystan's home.

"The night you thought me so drunk I could not speak, I was ill from watching The Others kill the Ancient trees and destroy homes of our friends. I couldn't stop being sick long enough to explain to you. When I finally got the horror of that picture out of my mind and stopped throwing up, you'd gone to bed--angry. I didn't want to disturb you."

Ailidh's face blanched and she slumped to the cloth-covered chair Kayne had so carefully carved from a branch the Ancient tree had gifted them.

"Wh-wh-why? We've not harmed them. Why do they want to rip out our homes and make us move?"

"I don't know my love, but we've got to find a way to fight back or we'll be next."

Kayne had soothed Ailidh's fears that night, but she began a campaign to move to Faetown and get out of the meadow and woods they called home.

Kayne sighed. She'd get her way and they'd move, but he wasn't going without a fight.

He felt a soft rush of air caress his cheek and looked up to find Ailidh alighting gently on her bare feet, her toes inflamed and angry looking.

He nodded to her. "Better get the Librarian to wrap those before they swell too much. Wouldn't want to put your *shoes* in the rubbish bin." Licking several fingers, he turned the page, the crinkle of the slick paper echoing off the wall of books.

When his smarmy comment met with silence, Kayne looked up to see a large tear meandering down Ailidh's cheek. He dropped the magazine to the table and hung his head, pushing out air between his lips. He'd done it again. He'd hurt the one woman who put up with his attitude and still loved him. Most women of the Fae would have kicked out his boastful self long ago not tolerating his pride and pomposity. Not Ailidh. She'd just look at him with those enormous sparkling moss green eyes, pat his hand and kiss his cheek. Kayne, unlike most Fae men, preferred one mate and one mate only. He never had understood the need to wing from inviting mossy bed to inviting mossy bed.

He reached out and grabbed the wayward drop heading toward the

6

fine line of Ailidh's jaw.

"I'm sorry, my love. Let's see if the Librarian has something to ease the pain." Kayne lifted himself from the chair and fluttered to the back of the building.

On the door was a sign. It read: "Rap loudly. Human hearing."

Kayne pounded on the door, settled himself on the floor, and waited.

Slowly the big door opened; before him stood a giant of a person. He sucked in a deep breath and felt his wings tremble.

Pulling up a stool, the giant Librarian sat. She was nearly at his eye level. A gentle smile touched her lips and crinkled her gray eyes. The essence of wild roses swirled lightly on the air.

"Kayne. How can I help you?"

Her soft voice purred quietly to his keen hearing.

Kayne opened his mouth but nothing came out. He coughed, stepped back then winged himself up a foot. At this level, he was looking in to the kind eyes.

"Ailidh... Ailidh has been practicing with those high heel shoes, and now her feet are swollen and hurting. Do you have something that would help?"

Linda thought for a moment. "I do believe I have something to ease her pain. I also have some Epson salts you can take with you so she can use them tonight. Wait here."

Rising from the step stool slowly, she walked to the back of the small room and opened a cupboard on the wall. Taking out a box and a bottle, the Librarian returned to the doorway.

"May I come out and administer to her?" Gray eyes questioned as she stood with the medicine in her hands.

Kayne hesitated. Ailidh liked the Librarian, but he still didn't trust her. After all, she was one of the Others. He turned his head and saw his mate trying to stifle the large tears meandering down her cheeks by swiping at them with the back of her hand.

"Yes. Please. She's in such pain."

Linda was surprised. Very few of the wee folk had become comfortable with her presence. Ailidh was the exception, so getting their permission to move about her own home was necessary if she was to keep them coming into her library.

"Lead the way, Kayne." She wasn't above playing to his male vanity.

As they got closer to the tiny faerie, Ailidh straightened in her chair and sipped from her coffee drink. She was a bit startled to see the Librarian out in the building. She didn't come out in the daytime for fear of scaring away the wee folk that gathered. Something must really be wrong for her to take such measures.

"Librarian." The sweet sound of Ailidh's voice carried to the odd pair approaching her.

"Ailidh. How are you today?"

"I'm well, thank you. What brings you out of your room?"

"Kayne asked me to see to your feet. He mentioned you were suffering and asked if I could help."

Ailidh shot Kayne a glare. "My toes are swollen and hurt a bit, but they will heal without help, thank you."

Linda could sense a fight brewing and opted to take the diplomatic way out.

"Well, let me give you some of my healing helpers. Use them if you like and if not, hang on to them. At some point in the future, they might come in handy. These little orange pills here relieve pain from the inside out, small dose aspirin. I believe you have this remedy in a leaf you brew; this is just easier to take and not quite so bitter. Just swallow them, don't chew, and in about 20 minutes you should feel some relief from the aching."

Linda gently shook the box of Epsom salts.

"These salts work if you place them in hot water and soak your feet. They're called Epsom salts and can be quite handy for those days when you've trekked too far. I'd be more than happy to get a tub so you could start the healing now."

Ailidh looked at Kayne's worried face and the concern on the Librarian's face. She pushed out a sigh.

"All right. If it will make both of you happy..." She watched relief flood the faces of the two people she cared about the most. If this would stop her feet from throbbing... she'd try anything.

"I'll get Chrissy to give you a hand." Linda took a step and hesitated. Turning, she asked, "Is that all right with you?"

Ailidh nodded.

Linda trod lightly on the old oaken floor. As she came close to the kitchen, she stopped, waiting until all her clothing had stopped rustling. She cleared her throat and closed her eyes. She'd made an agreement with the small ones to ask permission before peering directly at them--it was considered polite in their realm.

"Chrissy?" Linda whispered.

"Yes, Librarian?"

"May I speak with you?"

"Of, course, Librarian. Let me dry my hands and I'll join you.

Linda sighed quietly. These wee ones had taught her to slow her world down. It was a lesson she greatly valued.

The whirl of wings wisped past her face and she scrunched her eyes tight.

"Please, Librarian. I thought we had agreed we would not stand on the formalities. Open your eyes. I wish to see your storm-cloud colored eyes."

Chrissy maneuvered herself to sit on the hand railing that separated the kitchen from the main floor.

Linda relaxed her features and allowed her eyes to open; before her sat the tiny nymph. She had clad herself in a fifties-style, carhop uniform, ingeniously made from the petals of daisies and roses.

Linda allowed a smile to touch her lips. "You're looking very... official today. Any particular reason?"

Chrissy shifted her position. "Yes, I was reading on the Internet that servers used to get something called tips. Every server I saw had a uniform so I decided I like this style best and put it together. Maybe I'll get some tips."

Linda was finding it very hard not to laugh aloud. "Well, Chrissy, I don't really think you have a need for tips."

Chrissy pushed her lower lip out and furrowed her brow into a thunderous frown. "Why?"

Linda caught herself before a grin covered her face. "Because tips are paper money customers leave if they think the server has done a good job. Since you live here in the forest and most of your housing, food, and needs are met without having to buy anything, paper money doesn't really have any value, does it?"

Chrissy's lip pulled in and she smoothed her brow. Her face took on a quizzical look and she tilted her head. "I think you're right. Well, this uniform would be wilted by the end of the day, anyway. I'll just wear my regular clothes tomorrow. Was there something you needed, Librarian?"

Linda allowed herself a small chuckle. "Yes. Ailidh has injured her feet, and I wish to get a pan large enough for her to fit in both her feet. I'll need to have water warm enough to melt these salt crystals and then a towel available for her to dry her feet."

The little nymph narrowed her eyes and puzzled the situation. "I know there are some large pans in the very back of the cupboard. Will you come in and pull them out?"

Linda hid her surprise. She never entered the kitchen when Chrissy was working. Her size terrified the little nymph and it was, again, one of the agreements they had made. Moving very slowly, Linda entered the tiny room. She crouched on her knees and opened a very tiny door. In the back was a small, quart size, sauté pan which she was sure was the pot the little nymph meant. Using two fingers to slide out the pan, she pulled it from cupboard and placed it on the top.

"Is this the one you meant?"

Chrissy buzzed into the room and looked at the pan. "Yes. I'll warm some water in it in the microwave..."

"Uh, don't do that. The one thing that won't work in the microwave is metal. If you'll allow me, I'll find something plastic…"

Chrissy smacked her forehead. "Librarian, don't worry. I'll just have to use my magic. How silly of me to forget heating water is one of the first things we're taught. So, if you'll leave?"

Linda rose slowly from the floor and feeling somewhat like a pretzel, backed out of the small space. She rolled up to her full 4 ft. 8 in. height. It felt good to stretch her cramped muscles.

"I'll leave this to you, Chrissy."

Turning she noted Ailidh and Kayne deep in conversation. Something about the body language of the two wee ones was very wrong. It made Linda think. These two were not the only faeries to come into the library and whisper in frightened, muted tones. Linda was determined to find out what was causing such consternation among the Fae community. From the trembling of their wings, she needed to move fast or her tiny folk would be gone, and Linda would be alone with her library full of books.

Chapter Two

Linda crept toward the huddled bodies of Kayne and Ailidh. She stopped, her eyes cast down, and cleared her throat. Her ears picked up the rustle of wings.

"Yes, Librarian?" It was the melodic voice of Ailidh.

"I was wondering if I might speak with Kayne privately for a moment."

Frantic whispering ensued. Linda was hoping the two would decide soon as her neck was beginning to pain her.

"Please look up, Librarian."

Linda brought her eyes up to face the piercing forest green orbs of the tiny faerie.

"What do you want with my mate?" A tiny eyebrow slowly arched upward.

"There has been some unrest within the…" she hesitated.

Calling the faeries by that name could bring a world of problems on herself and the library. She frantically searched for the proper terminology.

"…the Hidden Ones' community."

Ailidh and Kayne smirked at each other.

"It's okay to call us faeries, Librarian. You have our permission." They saw her shoulders relax and she breathed a sigh of relief.

"I've noticed many of my patrons whispering in hushed tones and frowns have replaced the happy smiles once exhibited. I'm very worried and hoped Kayne might enlighten me as to how I might assist."

Chrissy arrived, carrying a towel-wrapped, steaming pan of water.

She placed the pan on top of the towel on the floor in front of Ailidh.

"There. I've brought some of the salts to sprinkle in the water once you've slipped your feet in the pan, Ailidh."

Kayne turned toward his mate. "I'm going to talk with the Librarian outside. I'll be back shortly." He kissed Ailidh lightly on her forehead and winged his way out through the open window.

Linda moved carefully toward the door listening to Chrissy fuss over Ailidh and her sore feet.

"What were you doing to get your feet so swollen? Oh, Ailidh, they must really hurt. Here, slip them into the water. See, isn't that better? Now, I'm supposed to sprinkle these crystals in... Ooohhh, look! They fizz!"

Linda allowed a smile to touch her lips. Chrissy had been a godsend in the small community. Unlike most forest nymphs, she was determined to be successful in a businesslike way and had welcomed the opportunity to work and be around an Other. Linda couldn't understand the little nymph's need to be human. She would've given her right arm to be a fae of the forest. Oh, well, seemed no one was happy with their lot right now.

Linda slipped out the door and quietly sat on the second step. Kayne had drawn up one of the chairs to the edge of the top step and was tipping the legs back.

"What is it you want to know, Librarian?"

"Kayne?"

"Yes?"

"Can you read?"

"Yes, Librarian. Quite well. As the first son, my parents made sure I was well educated. They felt having the ability to read the Others' language would help me to keep the community safe. I've tried to keep up with the news by reading the daily papers when I can find them."

Linda nodded. An old mystery had now been solved. When she and Donald had first moved here, their paper was tossed on the front porch. Out of seven days of a week, four of those days the paper would go missing. They never could figure out why. So Donald constructed a paper holder and set it at the end of the driveway. Toward the end of his life, the only exercise he got was to walk to the newspaper box and get the daily paper. They never lost a paper again.

"Good. It will make my request a little easier then. I've noted my patrons are very upset. They gather in clusters in the coffee shop and start discussing--something. I'm not sure what it is because if I venture out to get a book, all conversation ceases. I'm beginning to get hostile looks. From what few snatches of conversation I gather, there is construction machinery damaging your homes?"

Kayne turned his head and looked at this Other. Should he let her know what was happening? Would he be betraying his kind? What if she could help?

He weighed the options and decided.

"The machines, you call them bulldozers, are moving swiftly through our forest and homes. They seem to strike without a pattern. We're terrified and unable to do anything. We don't know how to make them stop." Kayne sighed. "I'm afraid we're all going to have to move to Faetown."

Linda blanched. Her faeries were going to leave the forest. She couldn't have it.

"Has anyone come close enough to read the name of the company on the side of the machine?"

Kayne flinched and pulled back. His eyes were wide, his jaw had dropped open and his wings began to beat furiously against the chair.

"Get close! Are you mad? Those machines would crunch us in a minute, and no one would know!" He shook his head. "No, no one has been close and I wouldn't ask anyone to try."

Linda waited for his wings to stop churning. When Kayne folded them against his back, she knew he'd settled down enough to broach him with her idea.

"I asked because if we could get the name of the company off the door of the bulldozer , then we might be able to check on the computer to see who owns the construction company. I'd be able to check official records to see what the project is requiring them to work so haphazardly.

From that point, we might be able to formulate a plan to stop the destruction of the Ancient Ones."

Kayne's eyes popped open. "You know of the Ancient Ones?"

Linda nodded. "I had many years to study before you wee ones showed yourselves to me. I know of the Ancients. It angers me to see them systematically destroyed for no reason."

Kayne shook his head. The librarian was amazing him with her revelations. She seemed so in touch with his kind, and he knew... well, nothing about her. He turned his deep brown eyes her direction.

"Why would you aid us? You're one of... them?"

He watched anger flash across the face of this Other. As quickly as it had surfaced, he saw it replaced by a kindly smile.

"I always knew of you wee ones. Before I married the Mr. and took his name as my own, my family name was O'Rourke. The little folk have long been welcomed in my family's homes.

"The cups and saucers, plates and silverware you use in the coffee shop were all forged and molded by my great, great, grandfather. Our hearth always featured food for the fae. I grew up with faerie..." she glanced quickly to Kayne at her slip of the tongue.

He smiled and nodded forgiveness.

Linda cleared her throat and continued "...friends. They didn't change--I did. As I got older, they seemed to disappear, and I began to believe seeing them had all happened in my head.

"Then we moved here. Chrissy was the first to show herself."

Linda smiled. The day she arrived had been a particularly tough one. Donald, her husband, had been so sick; Linda knew he wasn't long for this world. She'd had to make a decision to like living in the woods or sell everything and move back to San Francisco.

She had sat on the front porch--Donald having finally fallen asleep--and stared into the woods surrounding their home.

Suddenly, there she was standing on the top step, her wings poised elegantly.

Linda remembered holding her breath not sure the sight before her was real.

~ * ~

The two stared at each other.

The Librarian not daring to move.

The nymph not sure if she should speak, and when she did ,where to start.

Chrissy spoke first.

"Might I have a cup of coffee?"

Linda blinked and released the breath she'd been holding.

"Black?"

"Sugar and milk if you have it."

Linda nodded. "I'll bring it out. Have a seat."

She backed slowly toward her front door. Ever so gently, she opened the door and sprinted to the kitchen. She put a cup of coffee in the microwave warming the brown liquid. As she waited, she looked around for a container small enough to fit the nymph's hands. As she was beginning to panic, she remembered the tea set, forged by an O'Rourke hundreds of years earlier and passed from one generation to the next.

Moving quietly through the house, she went into the second bedroom and grabbed the set. She washed everything in the kitchen sink then filled the small coffee pot, sugar bowl, and creamer. Adding a cup next to her own porcelain teacup, she balanced the tray as she measured her steps to the outside.

She wasn't certain she would find the tiny wood nymph on her porch. She *had* been up for the previous 24 hours taking care of Donald. She could have hallucinated the tiny mite.

Upon opening the door, she spotted the miniscule visitor still seated on the porch. Noiselessly, she placed the tray on the top step, sat, and poured a cup of coffee for her guest, nodding her head to the sugar and creamer containers.

"Please... help yourself."

She poised her cup while the nymph doctored her drink. It wasn't until the little creature had taken a sip of her coffee that Linda spoke.

"I don't want to seem ungrateful but... what brings you to my home?"

She brought the cup to her lips and pulled a sipful of the warm liquid into her mouth.

"Because I need your help."

The liquid seemed lodged in her throat. Linda swallowed hard and looked at the tiny beauty. She cleared her throat.

"You need *my* help?"

Golden brown eyes reminding Linda of the bark of the oak trees surrounding her small home stared up at her.

The wood nymph nodded her head.

"One of the machines that the Oth... your kind uses came and tore my oak tree, my home, from the ground. I was down by the stream enjoying the day and dipping my feet in the coolness when I heard the screams of the yellow machinery. I hid myself behind a boulder near the edge of the trail running past my tree. If I would have been inside..."

The tiny nymph shuddered, her wings rustling to the very tips.

"...anyway--I was wondering if I might stay in the old oak behind your dwelling. I've checked and it appears vacant."

The tiny visitor looked so lost, Linda felt her heart melt.

"Of course."

The little visitor's shoulders dropped. "Thank you. And thank you for the coffee."

"I'll try not to disturb you. Do you need help moving in?"

"No. I'm carrying everything I now own."

The two sat drinking their coffee. When they had finished the pot, the nymph rose, her wings working lazily, and turned to Linda.

"You're different than most of the Others..."

"Linda."

"How is it you can see me?"

Linda watched the effort the nymph was exerting to keep herself aloft.

"Well…"

"Chrissy."

"Chrissy, as you appear to be very tired…"

The visitor bobbed her head in agreement.

"…why don't we save that discussion for another time?"

A slow nod of the tiny head, bobbing of the body, and the nymph winged to the end of the porch disappearing around the side of the house.

Several years and many cups of coffee later, the two had formed an unusual friendship.

Chrissy's home destruction was the first Linda had heard of the decimation of the Ancient forest and the homes of the fae folk. It was not, unfortunately, the last.

As the fae started to trust Linda, thanks to Chrissy's concerted efforts, and had begun to use the Lending Library, she picked up on the whisperings and saw the trembling wings more often.

~ * ~

Now she sat with Kayne hearing yet again another tale of unprovoked, wanton destruction of the ancient forest and fae folk homes.

Linda looked at Kayne. "If you can remember the name on the side of the dozers, we could use the Internet to track the owners. There has got to be a way to stop the devastation."

Kayne shifted on the step.

"I was trying to stay away from the machines."

Linda watched the color rise to his cheeks.

"I understand and I would have done the same thing. However, anything you can recall will help us to halt this killing."

Kayne thought for a moment. He closed his eyes and scrunched them tightly.

"I think I recall a triangular shield with a long sword crossing from the top left through the bottom right. There was also a name… black…

black catco. That's it. It was black catco."

Linda rose. "Great. Let's see if we can find some information about the company on the Internet."

"Excellent idea. A chill has begun to descend on my wings."

Kayne winged his way inside.

The librarian waited until the faerie had disappeared into the building.

Maybe, just maybe they'd get somewhere now. She hoped so. The daily razing of the forest was moving dangerously close to her home.

Like the wee folk, Linda feared the bulldozers... and like the fae folk, she had nowhere else to go.

Chapter Three

The setting sun spiked light off the gray circular tower of the multi-storied, river rock building covering two acres of the mountaintop. Wrought iron gates set in stone walls protected the summit fortress known as Citadel Saun from the rest of the world. The castle had overlooked the valley for as long as the residents could recall. Very few recognized the design as a direct copy of the Bothwell Castle in Strathclyde, Scotland.

Gitty stood in her dining hall at the long oak table. Chandeliers hanging on cast-iron chains from the 25-foot ceilings shed light around the long narrow dining hall. A crackling blaze in the man-sized fireplace emitted enough heat to warm the cavernous room. Strewn across the 16-foot tabletop covering the slab's magnificent wood swirls bordered in gold leaf, lay a topographical map of the eastern 25 miles of the valley closest to FaeTown. The tall, muscular night elf leaned over and drew large red x's on areas noted to be home to groves of oak trees.

"There's one less bunch of trees to search."

A sneer marred the fair face. Ice blue eyes pored over wavy lines showing mountains, rivers, valleys, and acres upon acres of wooded lands.

"That wretched little raisin of a leprechaun better not have lied to me, or I'll let Lancelot have him for dinner."

A 40-pound cat with glowing yellow eyes prowled its way around the leather clad legs of the elf. She reached down and pulled her pointed nails along the thick black fur of the animal's back.

"Soon, my love, soon."

Leaning closer to the paper, Gitty noted she was nearing the edge of the Ancient One's land and had yet to find what she sought.

"If we don't come across something soon…" She let the thought die.

The cat growled deep in its throat; the hair down the center of its back standing on end.

Gitty tried to ignore the cat's warning, but the sound of soft leather on flagstone disrupted her concentration and she looked up to see who dared to interrupt her.

"Oh, it's you." Gitty shrugged and turned back to view the map.

"Wow. Don't let your sisterly love overwhelm you at my return." Morgan strode his way to his sister's side and the map that seemed to have ensnared her constant attention.

"I just can't figure out the little raisin's rhyme.

'A stand of oaks

That all can see,

Hides the fortune

You seek from me.'

"I've bulldozed nearly all the oak groves in this valley and have yet to find the miserable little beggar's fortune. If I don't come up with it soon, I'll put him on the rack and torture the information out of his leathery hide. Then Lancelot can have him for dinner."

The cat yeowed at the mention of its name.

"That's right, my sweet, leprechaun for dinner."

Gitty traced a road with her fingernail. In her own writing, she'd drawn a house and noted, *Lending Library*. Directly behind the structure, per notes she'd written herself, was an enormous oak tree shading the building. The towering perennial housed several forest creatures and covered the building with shade in the summer. Gitty had dismissed it as inconsequential. She was beginning to reconsider.

"Maybe the leprechaun was playing with his words."

Morgan leaned over her shoulder and peered at the squiggly lines and circles on the paper.

"I think, sister, you need to get a hobby. This looks to be a child's attempt at art."

Gitty huffed her impatience. "It's a topography map, you idiot. If you weren't so busy trying to enchant every female that passes by you, you'd realize our time will be coming to an end very quickly if we don't find some sort of gold to purchase the land."

Morgan straightened and looked at the hunched back of his sister. "What in the world for? We're elves; we have no need for the things humans consider so important."

Gitty dropped her head to her chest and pushed out a sigh. "You fool. Of course, we don't *need* money. If we want to continue to live in this castle and keep the grounds human-free, we need to be able to purchase the land around it to stave them from our fortress."

Morgan's brow furrowed. "Why? No one *owns* the land. The land belongs to all who live in the forest."

Gitty whipped around, fisted her hands on her hips, and glared at her younger brother.

"You, mushroom brain, have been thinking with your sexual organ and not your head. If you'd taken the time within the last 100 years to notice, man has begun *buying* all the forest. Somehow they have found a way to own what was not ownable. If we don't use their paper money to purchase what was ours by rights, we will be thrown off our family's land.

"Are you going to go and get one of their jobs to bring in some of their paper money?"

Morgan pulled himself to his full 6' 5" of height. "I don't need a job. I'm elfkind."

"Well, elfkind, help me locate the leprechaun's fortune or you'll be elfkind living in a cave and bathing in the river."

Gitty resumed her position at the table studying the map.

Morgan looked at his older sister. She was not one to mince words. He thought about his latest ventures into the nightclubs of the humans. The females were drawn to him as bees congregated around the hive, but the moment they learned his looks were not attached to money, they disappeared. He'd spent more than one night in the company of some troll of a woman due to the lack of this paper money of which Gitty spoke.

Morgan moved next to his sister and looked at the map.

"The only thing I see is this place here."

Morgan's finger rested under the simple drawing Gitty had made of the Lending Library.

Chapter Four

Linda dragged her hand through her hair, scrunched her eyes shut, and tilted her head back. She'd been sitting in front of the computer for hours trying to track the business name Kayne had said he spotted on the side of the excavation machinery. What she located was a maze of business organizations bleeding into other organizations all circling back to Black Catco. No one seemed to own the company, and there was no paper trail on the county site indicating a permit issued to bulldoze the woods surrounding her home.

She sighed deeply and brought her head forward squinting at the stream of light spiking her eyes. Glancing at the clock on the computer, she moaned.

"God, I didn't realize how late… make that early… it was. I need sleep, or I'll be as grouchy as Simon Stockington on a good day."

Linda emitted a tired giggle. No one could be as grouchy as the ancient mailman. Feeling woozy and lightheaded, she left a note for Chrissy asking her to watch the library while she got some sleep. The destruction of the Ancient Woods and faeries homes would have to wait. Otherwise, her thinking capacity would be worthless.

~ * ~

Chrissy opened the door to a dark interior.
"This isn't good."
The bluish hue of the computer screen caught her attention and,

after flicking the switch to lighten the room, she allowed her curiosity to guide her. Taped above the computer display was a note from the Librarian.

Please watch the library today. Up all night researching. Need to sleep.

Chrissy moved the cordless mouse and watched the screen flicker to life.

"Oh no."

She sharply sucked in a breath at the image on the screen. Centered on the computer monitor was a triangular-shaped shield. From one upper corner across the face of the shield to the lower corner, a long blade was pictured. Above the sword and shield was the heavily printed word, *Black*, and under the image was one other word, *Catco*.

"Not again. I thought she'd left the area. Damn!" Chrissy muttered. "Tiamoon, you'd better be close by. We really need you now."

Turning off the computer, the little nymph trudged to the kitchen to start her day. She was going to have to call on the mice to get a message to the warrior gnome, Tiamoon. If Black Catco was in the area, the Lending Library was in trouble... as was everyone who lived in the surrounding woods.

Chapter Five

Ailidh tittered nervously as Kayne placed their luggage in the wagon. The dog pulling the vehicle shuffled in place, his actions bobbling the bed.

"Silas! Hold still!" Bram huffed.

"I'm anxious to get going. I'm only doing this as a favor to Ailidh, you know." The terrier mix turned to look at his business partner.

"I know, I know," Bram arranged the suitcases in the bed of the wagon. He fluffed the pillow on the seat and pulled out a blanket to cover the slender shoulders of his dainty passenger and her mate.

Ailidh winged to the front of the wagon and settled herself in front of the dog, Silas. She looked into his dark brown eyes and smiled. Resting her hands on his furry muzzle, she placed a tender kiss between his eyes.

"Thank you, so much, Silas. This is a tough move for us but knowing you care enough to take us there helps. Really, it does."

Kayne watched his mate work her wonder on the dog. If dogs could blush, he was sure Silas would be red to the roots of his fur. He figured to get things moving before it got too late.

"I think we should be moving before it gets dark. We have a long way to go my love."

Ailidh nodded but didn't move until she'd wrapped her arms around the dog's neck and squeezed gently. "Thank you."

She winged to the wagon and hovered over the seat next to Kayne.

He laid the blanket on the wooden bench and when she had set herself down, he wrapped the woolen spread around her body.

She shivered and leaned into him. "Let's get started. We have one stop to make before we leave the woods."

Bram clucked his tongue and Silas took off at a trot.

Ailidh and Kayne turned to catch one last look at their home.

"I sure hope this works out," she whispered to him.

"Me too."

~ * ~

Chrissy sat cradling the hot cup of liquid in her hands. It had been a long time since the *Black Cat* name had appeared. The last time the name had been uttered, the fae community was nearly wiped out. She couldn't--wouldn't--let that happen again. Tiamoon needed to be contacted; but how?

No one had heard from the warrior gnome in several years. After the last debacle, she'd left the glen swearing never to return.

Chrissy rolled her eyes. Kayne's brother, Keegan, had rejected every command the warrior had issued. His insubordination came close to undermining the defense of the woods and the inhabitants. Only after Kayne had thrashed him soundly had Keegan agreed to pitch in with the others and fight for their homes.

She felt the rise of panic. How was she going to find the warrior? Her reverie and questions were interrupted by the squeaking of the front door.

"Going to have to get that hinge oiled." She put her cup on the table. Standing, she blinked in surprise at the visitors.

"Ailidh, Kayne. You're here awfully early today. What brings you in?"

Kayne stepped toward Chrissy and extended a hand. "We're leaving the forest and wanted to stop by to thank you for helping Ailidh the other day. Will you let the Librarian know we've gone?"

Chrissy's mouth hung open. "Leaving, why?"

Ailidh looked at her feet, a shy smile touching the corners of her mouth.

"My sister invited us to live in Faetown with her. I've always told her no, but the other day when the huge yellow machine the Others drive nearly destroyed our home, well… " Ailidh lifted her chin, crossed her arms, and stood straight. "…I just made up my mind I'd had enough. I'm tired of living in fear. At least in Faetown my home won't be torn down."

She gave a nod of her head. "That's what my sister says."

Kayne shrugged his shoulders. "Where Ailidh goes, so go I. Thanks again, Chrissy, and please let the Librarian know how much we appreciate her help."

Chrissy pushed out a sigh. "Best of luck to you both. Send me news when you settle. I'll keep watch on your home--just in case things don't work out and you decide to come back to us."

Ailidh straightened her shoulders. "They will work out. I'm determined."

Chrissy cast a glance at Kayne. He was shaking his head slightly. She knew he would support Ailidh no matter the cause but recalled many an argument where he had been vocal about not wanting to live in the city. This change of heart meant Ailidh was very, very frightened.

The two faeries walked to the porch and down the steps to the wagon bearing their belongings.

Chrissy watched with a feeling of hopelessness as the pair departed.

I have to contact Tiamoon. Somehow, someway. The forest is in grave danger and we need a champion… the sooner, the better.

Chapter Six

Tiamoon paced the floor of her hut, the sound of her pliable leather boots whispering over the river stones. She couldn't sit still. She wasn't sure what the problem was, but she *just* couldn't sit still. This feeling of… restless dread permeated every pore in her body. She found herself whipping around at every creaking branch outside her window, jumping with every snap of wood in the fireplace, and in general, trying to escape her own skin.

Something was wrong in the forest; something was terribly wrong in *her* forest. She could sense it. A high keening carried on the drift of clouds pushed by the winds of the south filtered through the evergreens. The last time the woods spoke to each other in such worried tones, Mt. St. Helens exploded and killed many old friends. The feeling in the forest was taking on the same trepidation as it had in May 1980.

She stepped out her hut door and stood in front of her home listening. Restless trees swished their branches through the air, groaning in fear and expectation. The bushes rustled nervously and the only other sound was the throaty hooting of an owl searching for dinner. All else was silent--too silent.

Inside, she reclaimed her chair facing the fire. She bent forward and stirred the stew simmering in the pot hanging over the fire. The fragrant smell of cooked vegetables curled around her nose and her stomach grumbled at her.

"Yeah, yeah. Soon."

A quick dip of the wooden spoon in the pot and she brought the steaming liquid to her mouth receiving more complaints from her stomach. The hot tangy liquid burned the edges of her lips, and she blew across the top of the spoon to cool it. A second test proved the cooling to be a success, and she gulped the food down.

"It's cooked long enough. I'm hungry."

Tiamoon dipped her bowl into the mixture pulling the dripping wooden container toward her. As she was about to tuck into the stew, a scratching at her hut's door halted her progress. She dropped the spoon into the filled bowl, precious liquid splashing over the side. Rising from her stool, Tiamoon set her dinner down and stomped to the door.

"This had better be damned good."

She flung open the door and stared out at the dark night. As she was about to roar her anger at the wind, a tapping on her boot directed her attention downward. Standing before her was a mouse with a note clutched between its teeth.

Tia snatched the document from the creature's mouth.

"Thank you. My jaws were beginning to ache."

Tia nodded.

"I'm to wait for a reply."

Tiamoon stepped out of her warm home and glanced around the nearby woods. There was no unusual movement, nothing out of the ordinary; just an early spring wind blustering through the tree branches.

Stepping inside she motioned the mouse to enter.

"Sit next to the fire. I'll bring water and some food."

"That would be lovely. It's very chilly this evening."

Tia humphed an answer as she fetched a container in which to dip water from the pail. She pulled a small bowl from her cupboard and filled it with the soup which still bubbled in the cooking cauldron on the fire.

Her hostess duties fulfilled, Tiamoon sat in her chair and opened the message.

Forest facing destruction from unknown assailant. Need your help, again. Please come as soon as possible.

C.

Tiamoon crumpled the note in her hands.

"Why should I? The last time I helped they ignored my advice and exiled me off the land. I don't care if they all get pushed into Faetown and never have a home again."

"Beg pardon?" The mouse pushed aside its empty bowl.

"Nothing. It may take me some time to come up with an answer."

Settling itself next to the warmth of the hearth, the mouse replied. "Take your time. My bones need warming, and this fire is very inviting."

Tia finished her soup and dipped out another bowl as she tried to formulate an answer to the message that wasn't as bitter as she felt. She realized much time had slipped away as the mouse began to snore gently.

She threw several large logs on the fire, washed out the bowls, and crawled under the covers on her bed. The goose down comforter gifted her by the Valley geese held her body warmth, causing her eyelids to flutter and close. She still had no response for the mouse to take back but maybe a good night's sleep would bring the right words to her mind. Tiamoon sighed deeply and drifted into a restless slumber.

~ * ~

She rose from her bed and rubbed her eyes. There was something dark gray in front of her fireplace.

"What the…" she furrowed her brow as she tried to place the strange apparition on her hearth. Grabbing her boots, she pulled the supple leather over one foot then the other. She leaned to grab her sword from it resting place next to her bed and stalked silently on leathered feet toward the intruder. Her journey to the hearth halted at the piece of crumpled paper on the floor.

The sword slid quietly into its sheath on her belt, the events of the previous evening replaying in her mind.

"Oh, yeah… an answer."

Tiamoon grabbed her fur cloak from the hook by the front entry and braced herself for the chill and probable rain of the morning. She pulled open the door and found herself squinting at the brightness assaulting her.

"Wonders never cease."

She trod around the side of the hut and gathered wood to start the morning fire. Above her a formation of geese headed north squawking noisily as they left the approaching summer.

Hoisting the wood in her arms, she muttered, "Looks to be a hot summer."

She bobbled the load to the front of the hut and pushed the door open with her foot shoving it closed behind her. Padding to the hearth, Tia dropped the cut logs on the flagstones.

The gray lump stirred. From the mountain of fur a furiously moving nose and twitching whiskers appeared. Tiny, bloodshot eyes blinked rapidly and peered at Tiamoon.

"Ah, yes. I really can't thank you enough for allowing me to share the warmth of your fire and dryness of your hearth. Have you an answer to send back?"

Tia sighed. She'd like to tell them to handle their own problems; they were so certain they didn't need her the last time, but Fae Forest was her home. She was as tied to it as if the land had born her. Last night's message had put understanding to her restlessness of the last few weeks.

She watched Mouse stretch. Tia moved forward arranging the logs in the fire pit and set flame to the wood. The night's chill began to subside from the hut's interior.

"I have fresh bread baked by one of the local lasses in payment for a favor I did for her. Let's have some bread and water. After that, I'll give you a reply."

Mouse's ears perked up and his pink tongue slipped out around his lips.

"You know, you're not obliged…"

Tiamoon held up a hand. "I know. I also know it's better to work with a full stomach."

"That's true." Mouse wiggled himself as close to the fire as he could without singeing his fur. "Ah, but this feels good."

Tia had gone to her pantry to retrieve the bread and returned with a full bowl of water and thick slice of bread. "You'll be pleased to know the sun shines today. No rain to soak your fur."

Mouse's eyes brightened. "How wonderful! My senses tell me we are to have a long, hot summer."

Tia nodded. "The geese fly north as we speak."

As the two ate in silence, Tiamoon intently watched Mouse. He shifted and cleaned his whiskers.

"Have I dropped crumbs on my coat?"

Tiamoon stood. "No, no, that's not it. I think I may have a solution to you having to carry the message back in your mouth."

Mouse smiled. "That would be welcomed. I get so tired I have to stop more often than I should. Any help would be appreciated."

He watched her rummaging under her sleeping spot. All sorts of curious items emerged from beneath her bed until he heard her exclaim, "Aha! This is just what I wanted."

She turned and held up some kind of log-shaped item with a long string attached.

Mouse's eyebrows came together. "What is it?"

Tiamoon explained as she walked toward him. "This is an old quiver I haven't used for a very long time."

Mouse's frown deepened. "A what?"

"Quiver. It's used to store arrows when you are hunting and need to carry more than one with you. That's why it has a securing strap."

"Oh."

"I think if I extend the strap as far as it will go we'll be able to strap it to your back. Once that's done, we can put a message inside, create a cover for the end and you'll be able to travel without holding the message in your mouth."

Mouse sat on his haunches and smiled. "When do we start?"

"Let me reply to the note you brought me and we'll get things set."

Tiamoon padded to the cupboard where she stored her dishes and pulled open a drawer. Lifting out a pad of paper and a pen, she stood at the counter and formulated a reply to the note. She rolled the answer into a cylinder and placed it inside the quiver. Opening the second drawer of the stand-up cupboard, she located a knife. Kneeling down on the floor, she pulled the quiver to her and punched a hole in the very end of the leather holding strap. Next she got up and started toeing through the items on the floor she'd pulled from under her bed.

"There."

She bent down and pulled two items from the floor using her foot to shove the rest of the stuff back under the bed.

Mouse watched as she placed a piece of tanned leather over the opening of the quiver and secured it with a leather thong.

"That should hold everything inside. Now, mouse," Tiamoon turned to the messenger, "I need you to allow me to put this around you."

Mouse looked at the contraption, thought of his aching jaws the previous night, and nodded.

Tia slid the cylinder up his arm, over his head, and settled it between his shoulder blades. Noting it slipped easily, she moved back to her bed and got on her hands and knees.

"I know it's here somewhere." She reached beneath and pulled a long strand of leather to her as she sat on her knees. She looked at the strand then at the mouse with the quiver hanging off its side.

"I must make an adjustment."

The mouse sat back on its haunches.

Tia took the leather strand in hand and walked around the mouse. She stopped behind him and a smile began to slowly emerge on her lips. "Bingo."

"What?"

"I'll be just a moment. Don't worry if you feel tugging. I'm not doing anything that will harm you."

"I guess I just have to trust you." Mouse felt a tugging and heard a soft zipping sound.

Tiamoon stood in front of him with a leather end in hand. "Hold this please."

He grabbed the end and waited.

She had the other piece of the leather strand and standing in front of Mouse, grabbed the end she'd handed him and tied the two together. She adjusted the quiver until the cylinder was positioned squarely in the middle then she cinched the strand to a comfortable tightness.

Mouse patted the leather at his waist. "The missus says I need to lose some weight. Guess she's right."

Tia smiled. "Well, I'll never tell. If I had more time, I'd fashion this to fit more comfortably. For now… this will do."

Mouse wiggled back and forth, the cylinder on his back staying in place.

"I think this is great. I'll be able to move faster, keep up my pace, and get home sooner. I've no complaints."

Tia threw her cape over her shoulders, opened the door, and walked outside with Mouse.

"How long will it take you to get back to Fae Forest?"

Mouse considered for a moment, sniffed the air, and narrowed his eyes against the light.

"If I can find Grizelda's Flight Service, two days. If I'm on foot, a fortnight."

She nodded. "Well, be careful. All sorts of creatures are waking from winter's sleep right now."

Mouse hopped into the field, his gray fur disappearing within the tall grass.

Tiamoon strode to the back of her hut. She untied the cape and slung it over the top rail of the fence. Drawing her sword, she crept toward the first outcropping in the field behind her hut. Tia's senses tingled. The skin on her arms prickled and her ears tuned to the sounds of the land.

"It's been a long time, my friend, but your sleep time is over. Ha!"

She jumped up and jabbed a well-used straw dummy. The arms swung around wildly, a flail at each end with the ability to deliver painful, bleeding wounds. Tiamoon dropped to the ground under the swinging arms her sword clutched tightly in her hand. She crawled on her stomach until she was beyond the dummy then ran the obstacle course twice until her undershirt lay soaked against her skin. Pushing aside wet strands of her hair, she plodded back to her hut. She divested herself of her sword and heavy cloak. The wall at the back of the hut sported a heavy velvet curtain which Tia pulled back, to reveal a modern bathroom: shower, toilet, sink, and storage for towels and linen. She turned on the faucet in the shower until steam roiled to the ceiling. Dropping the last of her sweat and dirt-covered clothing to the tiled floor, Tia slipped under the scalding liquid allowing the water to soothe her aching muscles.

"I will not be run from my forest again. I may ache and pain now, but in a fortnight my body will be the weapon it once was. I can only hope you are the cause of this, Gitty…"

The mention of the name caused Tiamoon to shudder, even within the scalding cascade of her shower.

"…this time, you'll face eviction. I'll see to it."

Chapter Seven

Ailidh's head swiveled from side to side and up and down. She'd never seen such wonders as there were at this city at the edge of the forest where her sister resided.

"Kayne, will you look at how tall those buildings are. They must be the size of the old oak in the middle of the forest. I thought the Lending Library was big but compared to these… " Her green eyes resembled the saucers the librarian placed under her teacups.

Kayne narrowed his eyes. All he could see was the dirty concrete streets filled with trash floating in the light breeze which seemed to push them into town. There were strange vehicles parked near the concrete pathways and people seemed to be rushing around, their heads staring down as they quickly walked to and fro. The gray colored buildings *were* the height of the old oak, probably 50 to 100 feet tall in Others measurements. Unlike the oak, these monstrosities were dead, lifeless, and gritty.

"Yes, Ailidh, it's very different from the forest."

"I know. I think I'm going to love it here. There's so much happening and the town feels… alive!"

Kayne snapped his head to look at his mate. Her face glowed and she smiled as she hadn't in many a month. He couldn't remember her smiling like this since the Other's machines started tearing up the forest.

A pain touched his chest. He'd been gone less than a week, and he missed the smell of the meadow near their dwelling, the damp of the moss-covered streambed nearby, and the rustle of leaves in the branches of the tree above their home. He was here in Faetown because he loved Ailidh.

That was the only reason. Plucking up courage he didn't feel, he answered.

"I think this is going to be... an experience." He slipped her hand into his and gritted his teeth in to a smile. *For Ailidh.*

The dog and cart drew up to a curb in front of a tall brick building. Kayne counted ten sets of glass above extra large windows at ground level. The façade of the building was plain red brick with light gray accents. He noted the panes looked like eyes peering out at the world. In the center of the building at the top of the ten-step staircase was a set of double doors featuring etched glass casements. Kayne looked up in time to see one of the doors swing open and a faerie with blue-tinted dark hair fly down the steps.

"Ailidh!"'

"Cadhla!"

Ailidh jumped from the cart tearing her hand from Kayne's and ran to hug her sister. They were a contrast in color. Cadhla was dressed in a black long-sleeve shirt, black jeans, and black high heels on her feet; her blue-tinted, short-cropped, dark spiky hair shimmering in the light streaming between the buildings. Ailidh was attired in her forest clothing of grass green diaphanous skirt, buttercup yellow blouse, and bare feet, her blonde hair billowing in the breeze.

Kayne shook his head. How could two such opposite people have the same parents? The answer was beyond him.

The two girls jumped up and down hugging as they danced in the street.

"Come inside and see my place. We have about three hours before I have to go to work so we can catch up." Cadhla linked her arm through her sister's and led her up the apartment steps.

Kayne looked at Bram and Silas and shrugged his shoulders.

"I guess we get to unload the cart."

"Better you two than me," Silas said. "Soon as you're done taking stuff out of the back, I'm taking a nap. My pads are sore."

Bram started to grumble about good-for-nothing, lazy help as he moved suitcases from the cart to the sidewalk. He frowned deeply as Silas lay down when he and Kayne were finished.

"Useless mutt. If he didn't own sixty percent of the business, I'd fire him."

Kayne smirked, knowing Bram wouldn't know what to do without his business partner and best friend.

"I know what you mean."

The two men hurried up the steps dragging suitcases hoping to find the giggling faerie sisters. They barged through the doors and stood inside a lobby with ceilings as tall as an oak tree. Both men gawked at the ornate paintings on the walls and ceiling, gold accents glistening in the light of the day.

"Wow!"

"You can say that again," Kayne said.

"Hello?" Cadhla called to them from a square hole in the wall. She motioned them over and pushed her hand against the side of the opening until they'd dragged all the suitcases inside. Once she removed her hand, the wall slammed shut on them.

Kayne, Bram, and Ailidh started pounding on the wall.

"Open up!"

They stopped and gulped air as the floor started shaking and the walls groaned. Each one clutched their stomach.

"I feel like I'm going to be ill," Ailidh turned to Cadhla.

She smiled. "It's an elevator. Sort of a moving room. This is a faster way to get to my apartment than walking up ten flights of stairs."

She could see the confusion in their eyes. "I'll show you when we get to the top. I live in the pent... in the top of the building; similar to the top of the tree--the highest branch on the tallest tree in the forest. You'll see when we get there."

The floor shuttered and bounced and the feeling of movement stopped. The wall opened into a hallway with rugs all across the floor. The three forest faeries stepped tentatively on the carpet. When the floor proved stable, they pulled the suitcases out of the moving room and turned to watch the wall shut again.

Cadhla motioned them to follow her. She walked to the end of the hallway and opened a large door. The trio followed her inside, Kayne and Bram bumping into Ailidh who'd stopped in the entry. Before her was floor to ceiling glass showcasing the top of the city and the woods beyond.

"It's, it's so beautiful!" Ailidh dropped her suitcase and darted to the window. Her eyes swept the rooftops of Faetown and caught sight of the forest leading to the mountain. She could just make out the castle of the night elves. The sight made her quiver.

Cadhla had eased up next to her sister. "I know. If I could block out the castle, this view would be perfect--the tallest branch on the tallest tree, don't you think?"

Kayne cleared his throat. "Cadhla?"

She turned to see Kayne and Bram still clutching suitcases. "Sorry, boys. The room over there." She pointed to a doorway leading off the main area. "You'll have your own bathroom and there is a tiny kitchenette inside if you want to make coffee and snacks. I have a maid who cleans and a cook. I gave them the week off so you could settle in and get comfortable. Just put your things in there."

Ailidh hadn't moved from her spot. "Sister?"

Cadhla moved to her side again. "Yes?"

"How can you afford such a place? In the forest, there is no need for gold, but I imagine you must need it here." Ailidh turned to her sister, the mirth gone from the forest green orbs.

Cadhla cleared her throat and avoided Ailidh's gaze. "Don't worry about that. It's handled."

Ailidh dropped her voice. "We can't stay without helping you somehow. I don't know what I can do if you already have someone to cook. Do you want me to clean?"

"No! That's what the maid does. Don't worry about it right now, okay? Just get settled in and we'll talk about it later."

Kayne had walked up behind Ailidh and wrapped his hands around her waist. "This view is magnificent."

Cadhla forced gaiety to her voice. "Isn't it? See, over there is the city hall and there is the oldest church in town…"

Ailidh watched as her sister rattled on about the buildings, streets, and history of Faetown.

Bram stood at the front door, his hand on the knob and cleared his throat. "Well, I'll be on my way."

Kayne and Ailidh trotted across the large room to the door where she hugged him and Kayne shook his hand.

"Give Silas our thanks for the great care and smooth ride he took in transporting us. Do drive carefully, Bram."

Ailidh watched as Kayne reached into his pouch for coins to pay Bram.

Bram held up a hand. "I will take payment when I have returned you to the woods. Let's just say this trip is only half over. I will convey your thanks to Silas. We'll wait for you to contact us about the return trip." He leaned closer to the two. "After all, you are Fae of the woods and that's where you belong." Nodding, he slipped out the door.

Kayne grabbed the handle, jerked the door open, and looked in the hallway for his friend. He was nowhere to be seen. A smile touched Kayne's lips. "Been a long time since Bram used his magic. Guess he wasn't too fond of that moving room."

He closed the door and drew Ailidh to him. "I will take care of you, my love. I promise."

He placed a gentle kiss on her forehead. "I'm very tired and the bed in the other room beckons to me. I'm going to lie down. You and your sister can catch up without me."

Kayne slogged across the living area and disappeared into the room gently closing the door behind him.

Ailidh turned to find Cadhla gazing out the windows.

"I'm glad you took my offer to come to Faetown. The forest isn't safe any longer, Ailidh. I've heard rumblings about the destruction of the Ancients. I wanted to be sure you were okay and having you here with me is the best way."

"How can you know what is happening there when you live here?"

Cadhla turned to face her sister. "I have my ways."

"Oh, you're magicing."

"No. It's not allowed in most of the common areas of Faetown. I have… sources who kept me aware of the situation in the Fae Forest."

"Then you know just how frightening it has become. I don't know why someone would want to dig up and destroy the Ancients."

"It's more frightening than you can imagine, Ailidh."

Ailidh looked at the lines around the eyes of her sister. Something was not right about this place where Cadhla lived. Faeries did not show age and this human quality about her sister frightened Ailidh.

I must find out what is going on… but not tonight.

"There is much we need to discuss, and I urge you to take heed of my words. However, I suspect you are as tired as Kayne."

Cadhla moved to her sister's side and picked up the forest faerie's hand.

"Sleep well, Ailidh, for tomorrow, your world will change."

Chapter Eight

Gitty stood tall, pulling her shoulders back and holding her head high. She knew the human construction workers talked behind her back, but she paid them well enough that while she intimidated most of them, they stayed for the wages.

She'd learned from her grubbing gnome stepmother the value of money. While the faeries had no use for money and its power, the humans who were slowly taking over the fae forests put a high value on their paper with funny looking men's pictures on it.

Gitty had lived to see her stepmother try, and fail, to bleed her father of all his possessions. At the end of the last war when the fae and gnomes had succeeded in keeping the forest from the night elves, she swore she would get revenge. She'd gotten her half sister run out of the forest, but Gitty wasn't happy with that small victory.

Her father's wealth of lands and gold had been dwindling over the years, thanks in part to her narcissistic, spendthrift brother Morgan. The other culprits were these pestilent humans. Their belief that everything they saw belonged to them had eaten through the family's gold as Gitty had to buy back ancestral lands. She'd taken over the family wealth, sent her stepmother back to the underground hovel where her father had discovered her, and pulled the purse strings closed on her brother. The silence of her missing stepmother was filled by the constant whining of her brother.

If she had not stumbled across Thomas, *that obnoxious little leprechaun*, drinking himself to an early grave over the loss of some wayward faerie, Gitty might have been forced to sell the family's massive castle and surrounding lands.

But the gods had smiled on her. With a bit of the old leprechaun's magic turned on himself, she had been one drink from getting the *exact* location of his fortune. As it was, she was working from a poem muttered by a drunk, mere moments before his kin burst into the inn and rescued him.

She was nearing the end of her search. There stood only twenty more stands of oak between the treasure she sought and the titanium safe in her basement.

Gitty ran her hand along the brilliant, yellow earthmover. She trembled at the power the machine exuded as it sat rumbling, eager to start its path of destruction.

"What the hell is taking so long?" Speaking more to herself than anyone else, she stomped her work boots on the ground. Time was wasting while they waited for the inspector's go-ahead. And everybody knows-- time is money.

She turned to give her crew the thumbs up when her messenger came running and yelling with each step.

"DON'T START THE EARTHMOVERS! DON'T START DIGGING!"

He stopped in front of Gitty, panting and holding his side.

She crossed her arms and glared down at the underling.

"What do you mean, don't start digging?"

He had his hands planted on his knees, head down, gulping in great drafts of air.

"Like I said… don't start excavating."

Gitty bent over and locked her ice blue eyes onto his.

"Why the hell not?"

The young man gasped at the face before him. "Be… be… because there's been a 'cease work' order put on this site… on all this company's sites."

He straightened up and took a step back.

Gitty mirrored his actions. She watched his face drain of color.

"A cease-work order?"

The runner's mouth moved wordlessly reminding her of a fish on the riverbank. She pulled up to her full height and towered over him.

"Uh, uh. Somebody's filed a protest against this company. According to the inspector, until there's a hearing, nothing moves."

"Great!" Gitty smacked the side of the earthmover.

The young man jumped and started moving backwards.

"Ahhhh! Everybody go home!" She slammed both hands against the machine. The resulting boom echoed around the small valley. The human crew bolted to the four-door crew cab, the vehicle tires scattering rocks as they sped away. She checked the equipment, securing those machines left unlocked by fleeing workers, and trudged to her Hummer kicking pinecones with her boots as she walked.

How could anybody know who owned the company? She'd done her best to bury her name under layers of fake corporations just as she'd been shown. She was not going to let these human interlopers run her off land that had been in her family for centuries.

Gitty piloted the back road to her driveway and turned up the winding lane maneuvering the switchbacks until she drove through the gated entrance.

Looking through wrought iron bars into the valley below as she closed and secured the gate, she spotted the roof of the building the faeries called the Lending Library. She parked the Hummer in the converted stables and strolled to the front lawn. Standing in front of the massive stone castle on top of the hill, she planted her booted feet and fisted her hands on her hips glaring at the nondescript rooftop. Her self-centered brother Morgan had pointed out the obvious--the only structure left in her search area was the Lending Library.

"Those little faerie pains wouldn't know how to use the Internet, would they? What of the woman they call the Librarian? Does she have some human magic?" Gitty glared trying her best to magic an answer determined to elude her.

She started when the thought struck her. "It can't be, can it? Is it possible my dear stepsister is behind this?"

A wicked sneer marred the flawless face and lit the ice blue eyes. "I can only hope."

Chapter Nine

Linda woke with a start. The work she'd done ferreting out the owner of the construction company, who seemed hell bent on tearing down the forest, haunted her sleep. Every labored step had led down one convoluted quagmire to another false lead. It was a labyrinth designed by an expert--but not as expert as Linda at getting to the center of the maze.

She'd found Black Catco was owned by someone named Gitty Saun. More research had provided her with another entity named Morgan Saun and a Lancelot Saun. Land ownership records of the early settlers showed vast chunks of acreage in the area had belonged to the Saun family. Recently plots seemed to have been sold off at an alarming rate. Linda could only guess at the reason for the sales.

This latest flurry of movement on the owner's part was haphazard and sloppy. Her search had turned up evidence the Sauns were carrying on covert negotiations and buying the land surrounding the castle on the hill overlooking the small valley. Battlements were rising around the fortress at an alarming rate. Meadows shared by the community were being fenced with razor wire and charged with electricity.

Linda shuddered. Why was no one asking questions? Had the family bought off, or worse, eliminated their detractors?

She was glad her husband Donald had forced her to learn the ins and outs of the legal system. When he knew his health was failing, he'd pushed her to take over their business affairs. She'd hated the endless paperwork bog at the time and with his passing swore she'd never touch another form again. However…

Maneuvering the legal alleyways, Linda had been able to get a sitting judge to issue a cease-work order to the Black Catco construction company effectively stopping the forest destruction--temporarily. She, too, had been forced to hide her identity under blankets of deception, but the final results had been to waylay the earthmovers for a couple months. After the hearing… Linda shook her head.

I'm not going to worry until the time comes.

She dragged herself from her quarters, her slippered feet hissing quietly through the empty rooms of her Lending Library. She looked around. The book-lined walls felt strangely cool and foreboding. Linda realized there was no sound coming from the kitchen. She tread lightly so as not to scare Chrissy and announced herself before peeking around the kitchen door.

The room was empty.

That's strange. Chrissy is always up before me.

Linda decided to check on the nymph. Maybe she was ill and unable to leave her home in the oak tree. She grabbed a jacket from her room and headed to the front door. A quick survey out the window revealed no waiting patrons so she opted not to lock her door. She pulled open the windowed entry, turned left, and stopped in her tracks.

Beating her wings frantically against the wall of the house near the eaves was Chrissy. The expression of horror frozen on her delicate features stabbed Linda's heart. Reaching up as far as its black body would allow was a monstrous cat. At least that was what Linda figured it to be; whether it be wild or tame she wasn't sure. The creature was enormous and about to dig its claws into the aging wood siding on Linda's home.

"HEY! GET OUT OF HERE!" She stomped her foot on the wooden porch.

The creature turned slitted yellow eyes her direction and dropped front paws to the deck. It began to stalk toward Linda, a guttural growl growing louder with each padded step. As it approached, the animal barred gleaming, long white teeth as it wrinkled its nose and quickened its pace.

Linda kicked a foot in the animal's direction and, as the creature crouched to pounce, deftly sidestepped the subsequent attack.

The cat tumbled to the edge of the porch and, with her foot Linda shoved it over the edge, barely escaping the extended claws swiped at her.

"Chrissy! Quick!"

She opened the door and the tiny nymph shot into the house. Linda slammed the door shut and locked it. She peered to the front where the cat had fallen from the porch and noted the beast was sitting on its hindquarters licking the spot where her slipper had connected with its fur.

"What in the name of all faedom is that thing?"

Chrissy had fluttered to the nearest tabletop and was panting heavily. She pulled in deep draughts of air and closed her eyes. When her breathing had slowed, she opened eyes wide with terror and spoke.

"That is Lancelot Saun, the pet of Gitty Saun. "

Linda stared out the glass at the animal currently curling up in a sunspot on the driveway.

"That's a pet?!"

Chrissy nodded. "That's Gitty's cat. Gitty passes herself off as human but she is elfkind. Her family used to act as though they owned all the land between here and the mountains."

"According to the records at the courthouse, they did." Linda checked the whereabouts of the black cat again. It had not moved from the warmth of the sunny spot.

"Well, whatever, they demanded payment from all of the forest folk for living on their lands. We've been here longer. When the Fae council convened and decided they would no longer pay the ransom, the Sauns hired rogue elves to make trouble in the valley."

Wrinkles creased Linda's forehead. "When was this? I don't recall reading about it in the news."

"You wouldn't have heard of this. Humans were so busy with something you called a world war that our small grievances were of no consequence to you." Chrissy stood on the tabletop. She crept to the window and observed the napping cat.

"My father and brother were killed in the ensuing battles. Many fae folk lost family. The treaty the two sides signed held a clause exiling Gitty's stepsister, Tiamoon. Gitty was furious the gnome warrior had taken up the cause of the fae folk. She made the demand mandatory, stating if it was not carried out, the elfkind would slaughter all but their living within one hundred miles."

Chrissy sighed and brushed unseen wrinkles from her clothing.

"I really miss Tia. She was a good friend and a ferocious fighter. I would feel much safer with her here and not off in some distant land. I've sent word with the mouse network to the last place I knew she lived. I can only hope she still lives there and cares enough for some of us to come back home."

The little nymph's shoulders sagged.

Linda felt her heart ache for the little fae. She knew the loneliness of losing your best friend. Movement from the driveway captured her attention. The monstrous black cat was stretching all four limbs and looking as if he were going to settle in for the day. Something about his actions felt--wrong--to Linda. She could see his body quivering slightly, muscles ready to leap at a moment's notice. His head rested on his front right leg, eyes appearing closed, but she could sense they were opened ever so slightly and focusing on the Lending Library's front deck.

She watched the constant movement of his ears twitching back and forth. Linda had been so intently watching the cat, she'd closed out all action except the movements of the black animal in her driveway jumping when the loud clang of metal rent the air. She clutched the table the little wood nymph stood on.

"What the...?"

Lancelot jumped from his resting spot and arched his back, setting his hair on end, hissing loudly and baring his teeth.

Linda followed the line of his angry gaze to a small figure in full battle gear, a gleaming sword held high and to the right of its head in advance stance.

The cat hissed, crouched, and feigned attack.

The figure stepped forward switching the blade to the other side and advancing on the feline. The animal ruffled its fur to appear fuller, stood on the tips of its paws, and commenced growling.

The small warrior figure, body tensed, soft booted feet moving steadily forward, continued toward the creature.

Sensing the figure was not backing down, the enormous cat turned on its paws and fled across the driveway and through the meadow. The figure gave chase ,sheathing its sword behind it and pulled out a throwing knife.

Linda stared at the spot where the confrontation had just taken place. She couldn't wrap her mind around what she had just seen.

Chrissy strained forward trying to look sideways out the glass.

A face popped into the center of the window. Chrissy threw her hands over her face and screamed, the sound creating goose skin down Linda's back. Moving her fingers slightly from her eyes, Chrissy dropped her hands and screamed again.

"TIAMOON!"

Chapter Ten

Linda flung open the door and stepped back as Chrissy streaked past her to the figure on the porch.

The wood nymph threw her arms around a grim looking small person who grudgingly returned the hug.

"Tia! You came!"

Linda looked at her small friend. She'd never seen Chrissy smile so widely or beam so much as she was at this moment.

"Yeah, I came."

The voice from the small warrior was surprisingly soft, and Linda chose to stay where she was standing inside the doorway of the Lending Library.

"Come in, come in. You must be tired, hungry, and probably thirsty too."

Chrissy slipped her arm through the warrior's and led her through the portal to just inside the building.

Tiamoon stopped and gawked at the walls filled with books. Floor to ceiling on every surface were books; small books, large books, picture books, books of all shapes and sizes.

"When did this happen?"

Chrissy took Tia's arm and steered her toward a chair at one of the tables.

"Uhmmm, about 15..." she turned to look at Linda, her eyebrows raised in question.

Linda nodded.

"…years ago. The librarian and her husband lived here before that time but when he passed away, she started this." Chrissy waved a hand around indicating the shelving. "I've only been here for a year and a half in Other's time. My home was destroyed by the Other's machinery. They've destroyed homes of most of the forest fae and the meadow fae are finding themselves having a difficult time keeping their dwellings from being damaged. Kayne remembered the design on the yellow machine that tore up my tree and told the Librarian. She looked up the logo and discovered all the machinery belongs to a company Gitty and Morgan own."

Tia released the strap holding her sword and scabbard to her back and placed the gleaming weapon on the table. She divulged herself of two throwing knives and a hatchet she had worn on the belt of her hauberk. She hooked her thumbs on the collar of the protective shirt and pulled it over her head and off her body. Once divested of the warm, heavy gear she placed on a chair beside her, she sat at the table and looked around the room. After she had made a thorough reconnaissance of the room, she turned to the librarian still standing up by the door.

"This abode is yours?"

Linda nodded. "It is."

"How is it you can see us?"

Chrissy grinned. "She believes."

"Let me get you some water and a sandwich. Get comfortable and after you've eaten, we'll take your gear to my tree behind the house. It's probably the only oak still standing in the valley."

Chrissy winged to the kitchen and the sounds of water running and the refrigerator door opening and closing echoed in the empty library.

Tia watched the librarian.

"Why do you stand there?"

"I've learned to move carefully. I wait until invited before sitting with the forest folk."

"I've got a lot of questions. It's been many years since I left the forest and much has changed. Sit with me." Tiamoon nodded to a chair across from her. "My first question is why should I or any of the forest creatures trust you?'

"Tia!"

Chrissy flew to the table and alighting deftly near her friend, placed a container of clear water in front of the warrior. The gnome grasped the glass with both hands and gulped the contents in one swig. Chrissy raised her eyebrows. "Another?

"Please."

Tia looked at Linda who sat examining her fingernails. "My question remains. Why should I trust you? Have you bewitched my friend into believing what you say?"

Chrissy returned with the refilled glass and a plate with a sandwich she slammed on the table in front of the gnome.

"Labhoise Tiamoon Saun!"

Linda watched the face of the warrior darken. Eyebrows knit together and eyes narrowed.

"What did you call me?" She stood slowly, the chair legs scraping against the wooden floor.

"You heard me." Chrissy fisted her tiny hands on her waist and tapped a foot on the floor as she faced the warrior. "You know how careful I am. Do you think I would live anywhere near someone who would harm me?"

Tiamoon stood with her hands at her side, clenching and unclenching her fists.

"How am I to know? I've been away a very long time. Who knows what these Others have learned to do?"

Chrissy glared at Tiamoon who was glaring back at her.

Linda could see neither of them was going to give an inch.

"Ladies?"

"What?" They answered in unison.

"I'm very tired so I think I'll take a nap. Why don't you take some time and work out this problem together?" She rose from her chair and made her way to her room at the back of the library. She really *was* tired.

The confrontation with the monster cat had drained all her energy. A nap would feel good, and the two friends could discuss her at their leisure.

Chrissy crossed her arms, frowning at the gnome warrior standing across the banister from her. When the Librarian's door clicked shut, she huffed. "I would have thought you knew me better."

Tiamoon pulled a chair out and dropped into it. "Chrissy, how could you put trust into an Other?"

Chrissy rolled her violet eyes, flipped her light brown hair over one shoulder, and winged her way to the chair across from Tiamoon.

"You idiot. If the Librarian were a 'normal' Other she wouldn't be able to see us!"

Tia considered the nymph's comment. "Okay, so she can see us. That doesn't necessarily make her trustworthy, does it?"

"No it does *not*. But I've been living here for a nearly a year, ever since my Ancient oak was destroyed. She lets me live in the one behind the building. Tia, she knows the customs."

Tiamoon found two deep violet eyes peering earnestly at her. Huffing impatience, she acquiesced. "Alright. If you trust her, Chrissy, I'll keep my mouth shut."

The nymph smiled.

"I didn't say I would trust her--just keep my mouth shut about her. Now, what's going on here?"

Chrissy shook her head.

"Tia, it's been a nightmare. After you left, things were quiet--lonely but quiet. Gitty and Morgan kept to themselves, adding to that enormous house on the hill where they live. Time passed, and all those machine inventions starting appearing everywhere. Our forest started shrinking when the Others moved in and built homes. For the most part, we've kept to ourselves and life has gone smoothly. That is until about eleven moons, sorry, months ago.

"Huge machines started coming into the forest and killing the Ancients. Just tearing them up for no reason. They weren't even cut up for firewood!"

"My tree was the first to go. I gathered what belongings I could find and came here. I'd heard via the fae this human was different, trustworthy, and I needed to see for myself. She was able to see me; extended me kindness and understanding. Never said anything about my size or try to talk stupid to me like so many of the regular humans do. I asked if I could live in her tree out back and she said yes."

Tia watched her friend's facial expressions change with the story she told.

"So why are you working here, Chrissy?"

"Keeps me busy, and I like the Librarian's company. She's smart and helps everyone who comes through her doors. She's a good person, Tia."

Tiamoon scowled. "No Other is good, Chrissy. Don't ever forget that. So what happened to cause you to contact me?"

"Remember Ailidh and Kayne?"

Tia nodded.

"Kayne's brother's home was torn down about four months ago. When their home was facing destruction, Ailidh and Kayne started coming to the Lending Library to learn about city life; Ailidh's sister lives in Faetown. About three weeks ago, they moved away. They're not the first, and I'm afraid probably won't be the last to leave the forest to the Others and…"

Tia looked up to see the hesitation on Chrissy's face. "And what?"

Chrissy slowly blew out a deep breath. "…Gitty and Morgan. "

Tia raised her eyebrows high on her forehead. "The night elves? My dear stepsister and brother?"

Chrissy nodded her head. "The Librarian got Kayne to remember the picture and name of the company on the side of the huge digging machine. It was Black Catco. She got on the Internet and researched the company finally finding the main stockholders and owners to be Gitty, Morgan, and Lancelot."

"Mangy creature."

"That's when I knew I had to get hold of you. If anyone can stop

Gitty, it's you, Tia."

The warrior gnome smirked. "Thanks for the confidence, but I think I'll need as much help as I can get. Any reason for them destroying the forest?"

Chrissy shook her head. "No one has been able to figure it out. There is no pattern to the damage they do, but they're only tearing down the oak stands. Only a few remain. It was the Librarian who used the Other's laws to stop the digging up of the trees. She says this is just a temporary hold. If we can't do something quickly, Gitty will be able to continue digging up the Ancients."

Tia sat looking up at the ceiling and tapping a finger on the table. Finally, she looked at Chrissy.

"We need to convene the Fae Council."

Chrissy nodded her agreement.

"I'll use the mouse network to get the elders here then we can decide what to do from there." Tia nodded in agreement with herself. "I'll whistle for a messenger to deliver my requests."

She smiled at Chrissy. "Right after I eat."

Chapter Eleven

Kayne walked from the bedroom to the living area searching for Ailidh. He hated the long pants he was forced to wear and the leather shoes were causing blisters on his feet. However, he had promised Ailidh he'd try town living for three months. No more. If he hated it as much in three months as he did now, she had given her word they would return to the forest. He had to admit this penthouse, as Cadhla called it, did have advantages over the oak tree in the woods. He was getting used to warm showers and hot food on demand. Truth be told, he was also becoming quite fond of silk sheets. He felt himself stir with the thought of Ailidh naked on the soft sheets, her wings spread, hair cascading down the pillow…

Stop! We have to get to the job. He stopped on the step of the entry and turned to the windows.

There stood his mate facing the glass. Her shoulders drooped toward the floor. He noticed her beautiful, flowing hair seemed to hang limply and the sparkle from her wings was gone. In fact, she now kept her wings closed tightly against her body except at the job. Her delicate hand touched the glass and he heard a shuddered sigh leave her lips. He'd watched the fire leave her green eyes and her eyes had dark circles beneath them.

"Ailidh?" He spoke her name quietly.

The little faerie jumped.

Kayne watched her flutter her wings, lift her shoulders, and fluff her hair. She turned to face him.

"Kayne. How long have you been standing there?" she cocked her head to one side.

Danger old man. Don't push. "Not long my love. I think we need to get to the club. It's almost time for your first set. Are you ready?" He hoped the lie would go unnoticed.

Ailidh narrowed her eyes and pursed her lips. "Are you sure?"

He crossed the floor and gathered her into his arms. Placing a hungry kiss on her delicate lips, he tried to relay the love he felt for her through this action. Finally, he pulled back and stared directly into her face. "I'm sure. Are you ready?"

The two turned to take a last look toward the forest they loved so much. A sigh escaped Ailidh's lips.

"Yes. Let's get going."

~ * ~

Kayne pushed open the entrance to the cabaret, halting as smoke roiled out the door. He coughed, pulled in a deep draught of fresh air, and plunged into the dark, stale smelling interior. He hated having to work. He especially hated the way the fae men of the city leered at Ailidh while she sang.

Gareth, the owner, made sure the lighting on the stage highlighted her tantalizing figure through her diaphanous forest dress. When her sister had brought Ailidh in to meet him, as she had promised, Gareth's eyes glittered greedily at the nearly transparent garment and had made Ailidh promise to wear the dress solely for performing. He knew his clientele would pay to see innocence and beauty in such a package. He'd been proven correct. In the three weeks since Ailidh had been featured at the cabaret, business had tripled.

Tonight was putting Kayne's patience to the test. Twice he'd had to pull men from the performing stage as they lunged at his mate during her performance. Ailidh was in tears the last time.

"Kayne, please," she'd wept into his shoulder.

He'd just tossed a drunken, swearing gnome out the door as the creature had gotten close enough to lay his grasping hands on his mate's delicate breast.

"Take me back to the apartment. I'll talk with Cadhla, and we'll find another way to make money to give to her. Please!"

Kayne had helped her from the stage, protectively holding her trembling shoulders, down the hallway to the performer's area when they encountered a furious Gareth, arms crossed over his muscled chest, feet wide and planted, blocking access to the rooms.

"Where the hell do you think you're going?" The faerie's face was crimson, puckered, and glistening with sweat.

"I'm taking my mate home. She's too delicate to put up with the rude actions of your customers. Aren't there other places for the things they insinuate to Ailidh? I've heard you and Cadhla speak of such abominations."

Ailidh quivered beneath Kayne's grasp, a suppressed sob escaping her lips.

Gareth sneered at Kayne. "The only reason Ailidh is not working there is because her sister garnered my promise, on a 5-year contract, she wouldn't. How the hell do you think you and your 'mate' are able to stay in such luxury? Most forest fae who show up in the city eventually wind up living down by the river in hovels that make their oak trees look like castles. You are lucky your mate has a beautiful and willing, sister."

"Get Ailidh back on the stage before those blighters out there tear the place apart. Getting groped is part of her job, and she needs to act like she likes it!"

Gareth dropped his arms to his side and clenched his fists.

Kayne glared at his opponent. Gareth's three-foot form towered over him and he was not in the position to take on the larger man. His mouth pulled to a single, angry slash, his jaw setting tightly. He felt his wings flush red. He drew himself to his full height and pulled a trembling Ailidh closer to his body.

"I'll not expose her to that humiliation."

"Oh, yes you will," Gareth walked up and placed his hands on the tiny faerie's breasts.

Ailidh gasped and stepped backwards, Gareth keeping pace with her. Kayne's arm was wretched from her shoulders.

"I own these and everything else that goes with them. I'll touch them, the customers will touch them, and if someone pays me enough..." he let the suggestion die.

Gareth fondled Ailidh as Kayne watched all color leave her face. Her wings quivered and several emotions crossed her pale face.

The tall faerie then placed his hands on her shoulders and propelled her down the hallway and back to the stage.

The crowd applauded and yelled lewd suggestions. The microphone crackled as Kayne heard Gareth's coarse laugh. His stomach rolled with the realization he'd been unable to stop Gareth and protect his mate.

"Isn't she something boys?"

There was thunderous applause.

"And look as these perfect domes of womanhood..." The floor shook with the beating of shoes on wood. "Why don't we get this little beauty into our spotlight and have her sing us a tune?"

Applause drowned out anything else the owner may have said.

Kayne felt the heat of anger flush his face. He strode to the wings of the stage and watched as Gareth's large hands stroked from shoulders down to the buttocks of his beloved. As he started to charge the stage, two pair of strong hands restrained him.

"Don't."

Kayne turned to glare at his mate's sister on one side and a muscular dwarf holding him on the other side.

"She'll get over it and neither of you wants to live in the hovels down by the river. Gareth is crude but generous with his money when you understand he is the boss and his word is law. Once you resign yourself to that fact, everything gets easier."

Kayne strained against the hands.

"Please don't. He'll turn her over to the hospitality house owner." Cadhla shuddered. "She WON'T survive... the worst sort of lowlifes go there. Do you have any idea what they do to the likes of a faerie as beautiful as she?"

Kayne jerked his arms from the two as the breathy, whispering voice of Ailidh drifted through the microphone over the smoky room. The cacophony subdued and the sweet voice continued to strengthen with each sung note. He watched his delicate mate pull her shoulders back, lift and spread her wings wide, and stand straight, her chin held high. A strength he'd never seen in the forest seemed to fill her. By the end of the song, she'd stepped full into the spotlight, her diaphanous clothing disappearing in the strong glare.

A fae man weaving and sneering lopsidedly made his way to the stage. He reached a hand up to place it on the thigh of Ailidh. Kayne sensed rather than saw the shiver run through her but she leaned over, looked directly in the eyes of the drunk fae and spoke very quietly, her lips barely moving.

Kayne watched the drunk leer then, without warning or a visible move on Ailidh's part, he staggered backward.

Gareth scurried over to the customer. He frowned, nodded, and pointed a finger at Ailidh.

She stood tall, smoothing the fabric of her dress and tossing her hair over one shoulder.

Kayne, Cadlha, and the dwarf watched as the customer back stepped to the bar shaking his head and pushing Gareth away from him.

Cadlha turned to Kayne. "She is stronger than you can know. Someday I will tell you just how strong but not today. I told you she would do fine." She turned to her companion. "Turner, we have work to do."

Kayne watched his mate glide from the spotlight to the stage wings, a spark of fire dancing in her eyes as she caught sight of him.

Uh oh. I think someone is in trouble and I don't think it's me.

Ailidh strode with surety past him.

"Come on. We've got packing to do. I won't be treated like this. It's high time I started behaving as my true self."

Kayne found himself scurrying to keep up with his mate. Something about the set of her mouth and forward thrust of her step kept him from asking the thousand questions in his mind.

Ailidh grabbed her few belongings in the dressing area. She burst from the door and marched to the adjoining room barreling her way through the portal.

Cadhla's started at the intrusion. "What…"

Ailidh held up her hand.

Kayne noted there was no quivering, no shaking visible.

"I need you to call the person in your building who will let us in the apartment."

Cadhla leaned back in her chair and cocked her head. "Now why would I do that?"

Ailidh placed her hands on the desk and moved to within inches of her sister's face. "Because if you don't, I'll invoke the ancient spell."

Kayne watch all the smug leave Cadhla's face. She picked up the phone and called someone at the building where they'd been staying. Hanging up the phone, he watched her eyes as they swept over his mate.

"If you leave, I'll be locked into this contract with Gareth for five long years, Ailidh. You don't want me to suffer, do you?" Cadhlas' eyes darkened with the question. She unconsciously twirled a wayward strand of dark curls around a finger.

Ailidh straightened and stared down at the only living sister she had.

"You chose this path not I. Nowhere in your flowering invitation to visit the city was there a mention of the degrading job you arranged for me." Stealing a glance at Kayne, she lowered her voice. "I'm a warrior, Cadhla, not a trollop. That was a role you chose during the wars, not I."

Cadhla rose so quickly from her chair it tumbled to the ground.

"How dare you! I chose not to fight because I didn't wish to die! I was never any good with a sword, and you know that. I was good at… at… making things run smoothly." Steel gray eyes flashed dangerously, the ceiling light highlighting her blue streaked hair now flying freely about her face.

Ailidh planted her feet and crossed arms in a stance Kayne had not seen since he'd come into the tiny fae's life.

"I've been listening to the gossip from the customers these last three weeks. There is trouble in the forest and many fae are fleeing in fear of their lives. I will not stand by idly singing to drunken dwarves, city fae men, and what-all else while some outside force takes over my homeland. This life is yours, Cadhla, not mine. I belong in the forest--not this squalid mud bog you call the city. Don't get in my way, sister, or you will regret the day I arrived."

The tension in the room crackled, each sister squared off ready to battle the other.

Cadhla made the first concession. "I'll not stop you. I also won't stop Gareth if he seeks to find and bring you back."

Ailidh humphed at the suggestion. "You know of what I'm capable. Do you really think that gargantuan, lusting fool can capture me?"

"No. I'm just warning you he might try."

"Let him." Ailidh turned to find Kayne a step away from the door. "We're leaving."

Ailidh blew past Kayne and strode out the side door to the street, Kayne hurrying to match her strides.

Getting in the apartment proved no problem, and the couple thanked the doorman for his assistance. Once inside they moved to the bedroom closet.

"Is there anything here you need?" Ailidh stood with the door open gazing at the clothing they'd needed for town living.

"The sooner I'm done with these city clothes the better."

She looked at the clothes hanging in the closet and the shoes she'd learned to walk in and nodded her head. "Me, too."

Kayne had moved to the balcony off the bedroom and leaned on the rail gazing at the view from this vantage point. He glanced down at the street.

"Ailidh!"

"What?"

"Are we ready to go?"

"Yes, why?"

"Gareth just walked in the front door in a very big hurry."

Ailidh dashed to the balcony and peered down. Glaring up at her was Turner, the dwarf.

She pulled back and looked at Kayne.

"It's been awhile but we're going to have to use our wings."

Kayne took a deep breath and nodded.

Ailidh closed the sliding glass door, grabbed Kayne's hand and they jumped from the balcony spreading their wings and heading in the direction they had come from three weeks earlier.

Chapter Twelve

Gitty paced in front of the living room windows that overlooked the valley. Since Lancelot had come streaking back to their home several days ago, she couldn't get him to sit still long enough to magic what had made him so agitated. Seeing him on edge and not knowing why made her jumpy… and testy. All she could do was walk off the feeling until the wretched animal would allow her to see what had spooked him so badly.

Morgan breezed through the living area toward the front door his evening cape fluttering behind him.

"I'm going to use the Hummer today. I'll see you when I get back… whenever that is." He flipped a hand over his shoulder in a weak wave and made to grab the keys sitting in the crystal dish centered on the oak sideboard in the entry.

Gitty reached the bowl before Morgan had uttered the last word.

"No. You're not taking the Hummer, or the truck, or the Corvette, or any of the vehicles in the garage. You haven't earned the right to drive any of them."

He pulled himself to his full height and glowered down at his sister.

"I'm part owner of the company and because of that fact, I can drive any vehicle I choose. Move away from the sideboard."

Gitty distributed her weight evenly on her feet, ice blue eyes locked onto her brother's and fisted her hands on her hips.

"Our father was stupid enough to think you would actually learn to like working. He may have forced me to list your name as part owner of the business, but he can't force me to share the rewards of my hard work.

When you put in a full forty hour week working, real work, not wooing some bimbo in a bar to take you home, then you'll get the privilege of driving. Not until then."

The siblings stood face-to-face, daring the other to make the first move. Morgan finally tossed his head, turned, and started toward the game room.

"By the way, I heard a rumor our stepsister is in the valley."

Gitty sucked in a breath. She bolted after him and, grabbing his arm, turned him to face her.

"What did you say?"

Morgan smirked at her. "What? I know something you don't? Well, well."

She punched his shoulder. "Tell me what you heard."

He rubbed the spot where her fist had met his muscles. "Ow! That hurt. I'm not sure I want to tell you now." He feigned a pout until he saw the smoldering fire in Gitty's eyes.

"Oh, all right. I was at one of the taverns in town…"

Gitty rolled her eyes. "Morgan, just bottom line it for me."

He stopped, narrowed his eyes and stared at her. "This is my story. I'll tell it my way. Clear?"

Gitty huffed out an impatient breath. "Fine. Just get to the point sometime today."

"Anyway, as I was saying," he shot her a veiled glare, "at the tavern nearest the forest edge, I think it's called Dew Drop Inn or something stupid like that…"

Gitty closed her eyes and shook her head.

"…I wasn't having much luck finding a friend for the evening so I decided to move on from there. I stepped outside and nearly crushed one of those mice who work the message network they have. I wouldn't have known he was anything more than a common field mouse except he spoke to me. I wonder how he knew I'd understand?" Morgan frowned slightly.

Gitty stood looking at her 6'5" brother; his white hair glistening in the light from the front window, blue eyes framed by white eyebrows and lashes knitted together and shook her head.

He's such an idiot.

"Morgan?"

"Oh, yes. Well, he told me they were being kept very busy since Monday…"

Gitty whipped her head in the direction of the sleeping Lancelot. The cat opened one eye and turned his head from her.

"…running all over the valley delivering messages. I asked him if it was something I might be interested in, and he shook his head. Told me some gnome had just arrived in the valley and was in contact with family members, that's all. I mean; we know how they multiply like rabbits. After all, remember the family gathering when I was…"

"MORGAN!"

He jumped at the shouting of his name.

"No need to get all huffy. I asked if he knew the name of the gnome and the mouse nodded, saying it was something about a moon. I deduced the rest. Tiamoon is in the valley and contacting her family." Morgan nodded his head and smiled.

Gitty pushed a big sigh through her lips. "You're an idiot but a useful one. Here."

She tossed him the keys to the Corvette. "Don't scratch it."

He allowed a sly smile to cover his lips as he walked toward the garages. "I wouldn't dream of it."

Gitty wandered back into the living room to stand looking out the picture window. She took in the view of the valley below and let her mind travel back to a time when the woods were full of fae folk. Her family had been generous enough to let them live in the woods they owned and what had it gotten them? Whining, gripping tenants who complained about a little rent. They'd even had the nerve to threaten a war!

On top of all that fuss, her father had moved a wretched gnome woman and her daughter in with Gitty and Morgan. Gitty never understood his fascination with the little creature. She was certain the blasphemous being had bewitched him at some gathering they were always having.

Served him right when she left. Never trust a gnome.

So Tiamoon is back in the valley and networking with her family. Hmmm.

Gitty voiced her thoughts. "Thinking of starting another fracas, my sister? Feel free to try; it won't do you any good but please go ahead and try. It's been many a year since I was able to wade into the middle of a good fight. I'm actually missing the action."

Her hand ached to hold the sleek weighted blade, fingers wrapped around the handled designed specifically for her. Maybe, just maybe, she could rid herself of this stunted blight once and for all.

Gitty smiled. She rolled her head and shoulders trying to ease the tension that seemed to build daily. While the eflkind were superior to any other beings living in the area, the treaty which bore her signature along with her father and brother's signatures still restricted all the night elf community from using their magic to take over the humans. Tiamoon had just broken part of the original agreement by showing up in the valley. Gitty allowed a smirk to touch her lips.

"You set the ground rules, Tia. Only this time, I'm finishing the battle. You won't live to be banished. Once you're dead, the old treaty will only be good as fodder to start a fire. It's time for the night elves to move out of the shadows of the mountains and forests and take our rightful place in the world."

Gitty gave the valley one last look before heading to the basement. She followed the steps down to a hallway that ended in a large room featuring three walls lined in mirrors, a floor with rubberized matting as covering, and the fourth wall of floor to ceiling windows allowing natural light to stream in and bounce off the silver and black gym equipment.

"The fools who idled my construction company may think they have beaten me, but I will make use of this time and turn their foolish decision against them." She glanced around the room surprised at the cleanliness of the area. Morgan was not known for picking up after himself. She wrinkled her nose at the faint aroma of stale sweat and wandered to the changing area. Once attired in workout togs, she moved toward the free weights. She lifted a 20-pound barbell in each hand and began curling them to her biceps. Physical labor always improved her thinking. At the moment, she was faced with two major challenges; one-finding out what her stepsister was up to and stopping her; and two-finding the leprechaun's treasure.

"If I dispose of Tiamoon, I might not need the leprechaun's treasure."

Gitty clunked the hand weights down on the stand and stared at her image in the mirror.

"Of course! With Tia out of the picture, the agreement is void releasing me from peaceful behavior toward non-elfkind. I won't need the leprechaun's treasure. I can grab all the property in the valley, and no one will be able to stop me."

She smiled at her reflection.

"Some days I amaze myself."

Chapter Thirteen

Kayne dropped to the ground on the balls of his feet then fell to his hands and knees. Ailidh floated down beside him.

"What's the matter?"

He panted heavily, his head bobbing with each breath.

"I--haven't--flown--that--much--in--several--years."

He pulled up to rest his weight on his knees and heels, toes tucked under his bottom. Forcing himself to pull in deep draughts, Kayne slowed his breathing and heart rate. "I'm so out of shape. I've gotten lazy."

Ailidh looked at her mate resting on the ground. "We've both gotten lazy. I allowed you to make all the decisions and think I was...fragile. I'm done with that. My home is in danger, and I'll not trust anyone else to protect the forest but myself."

Kayne peered sideways at his mate. Her arms were crossed defiantly, legs planted on the ground as she rested her wings against her shapely back. Her alluring figure was barely covered by her diaphanous dress. Even with the intimate knowledge of what lay beneath the flimsy fabric, Kayne realized his fragile flower of the forest was gone for good and the temptation to suggest a quick interlude withered in his mind. The creature that had pushed him from the balcony in Faetown wouldn't succumb to his male vanity with fluttering eyelashes and a shy smile. This Ailidh was one he'd never known. The strength she had exhibited in the crisis surprised him considering her timid reaction not but an hour earlier. Something about the drunken male fae staggering to the stage had triggered a power from deep within his mate.

He considered her profile. He was going to enjoy this strong female. But would it last?

"What about your sister, Cadhla?" Kayne rose from the ground and approached Ailidh.

Ailidh pushed out a humphing sound. "I have no sister."

Kayne raised an eyebrow. To this point, Ailidh had spoken continuously about the older sister who had succeeded in the city; how smart, bright, and wonderful she was. This turnabout was... unexpected.

"Any being who would sell another doesn't deserve respect or a family. As of this morning, my sister ceased to exist." Ailidh looked around and pulled in a deep breath. "The forest smells so clean." She looked at Kayne. "Let's go to the Lending Library. I'm sure the Librarian can help us find a new home."

She started down the road, Kayne trotting to keep up.

Within the half hour, the two faeries spotted the familiar lane leading to the Lending Library. Ailidh stopped and gazed at the building, a mixture of elation and concern filling her.

"Do you notice anything?"

Kayne narrowed his eyes. "Not really. Why?"

"Where is everybody?"

He looked again at the front porch of the white building. Ailidh was right. Normally, on a day like today when the sun opted to appear from beneath the clouds, there were several fae outside sipping those coffee drinks Chrissy made, and the door was opened allowing fresh air to dissipate the closed-up smell. He couldn't sense his kind anywhere within a quarter mile radius. There was movement within the building and the essence of the Librarian and Chrissy wafted on the air. There was also another essence. One that was familiar but...

Ailidh snapped her head his direction. Her eyes were wide, sparkling with joy.

"Tiamoon! I sense Tiamoon."

She started to run then spread her wings and flew to the front door. Kayne followed, groaning with the ache his wing muscles produced. He touched down on the porch a mere seconds behind Ailidh. Her hand was already pushing open the Library door.

~ * ~

Tiamoon sat, her chin resting in the palm of her hand, staring out the window down the lane. Chrissy had made up a spot in the oak tree for her that she appreciated, but the inactivity of sitting around was irritating her. She really needed to practice her skills if she was to have a chance when facing Gitty. The thought put a smile on the warrior's face. She was sure she could convince the council to allow her the opportunity to face her detractor.

Movement at the end of the lane derailed her daydream. She strained her eyes to see if she could spot the movement again. At the beginning of the turnoff to the Library were two small figures trudging toward the building. Tia noted the two appeared to be fae in stature. She wondered if it were someone she might know. The figure wearing a flowing garment stopped then was suddenly flying up the road.

"Chrissy! Someone's coming up the driveway."

Tia stood up, feeling the rush of adrenalin pumping through her veins. Her fingers twitched over her knife blades, and she flexed her legs in anticipation of a confrontation. She could hear faint shouting from the flying figure. Her mouth went dry and she waited for the right moment to jerk open the door and meet the intruder head on.

She peeked out the window and saw two figures flying directly toward the Library.

As the two neared, Tia realized she was looking at Ailidh and Kayne. A gentle thudding indicated the fae had landed on the porch. Tiamoon opened the library door to find herself enveloped in the slender arms of Ailidh. Kayne dropped into the nearest chair on the porch, his wings quivering with exhaustion.

"TIAMOON!" Ailidh hugged the tiny gnome warrior tightly.

"Ailidh," Tia gasped for air. The little fae's small size belied her strength.

"Oh, I'm so sorry." Ailidh let go of the warrior and danced around her. "You're here, you're really here."

She clapped her hands in glee. "I'm so glad. Now everything will be just like it was before Gitty sent you away."

Tiamoon straightened her tunic and cleared her throat. "No, Ailidh, things won't be the same. Gitty has more knowledge of the magic and has had years to practice its use. She is more dangerous and cunning than before the war. I can only offer my help but will do my best to save our land. However, I have sent word for all the clans to gather. The decision to proceed must be made by everyone who has something to lose in the valley."

Tia turned to Chrissy. "Would the Librarian represent the Others?"

Chrissy thought for a moment. "I believe she would."

"Then what we must do now is wait for the mouse messengers to bring back replies to my requests for a council meeting. The decision for action will be made at that time."

~ * ~

Gitty stood at the front window staring down at the roof of the Lending Library. It seemed she spent a great deal of time in this spot contemplating her fate since the court had closed her work sites. The atmosphere of magic was building; she could sense it in the air, a light buzzing that tickled her ears.

"Tiamoon is back. Lancelot has finally allowed me to see his confrontation with her. But there is more to this than just her presence. This sensation feels more and more like the forest before the war."

"What are you muttering about, dear sister?" Morgan sluffed into the living room and flopped on the couch, throwing one leg over the couch's arm. He bit into an apple. The pungent sweet aroma of the fruit combined with the loud crunch disrupted Gitty's attention.

She turned in time to witness juice running down her brother's cleft chin. He swiped at it with a sleeve and crunched away. His lackluster eyes and drawn expression along with the listless position he took on the couch grated Gitty's nerves. At the best of times, she could barely tolerate his presence but now, with the company shut down, she was ready to kill him.

"Don't you have some young thing to impress?"

"Naw. All the local girls know I don't have any money, and if I want to go out of town, I'll need to borrow some cash from you."

He shot her a lazy grin then bit into the apple again.

"When you put in a decent day's work, you'll get a decent day's pay. Since my construction sites have been closed down, you're just out of luck." She pushed him out of the way and sat on the end of the couch. "Have you noticed, brother, the magic level has spiked in the last few days?"

Morgan laid his head on the back of the couch and stared at the ceiling. "And this would interest me because…?"

"Because, you oaf, our dear stepsister is in the valley and must be gathering some of her little friends together. Can't you feel the difference?"

Morgan pushed out a sigh as he pulled himself to his feet. He turned to his sister.

"I've noticed, but why should we care? They can gather a thousand of those stunted, miniscule creatures and still not have the power we have. So what's your point? Are you afraid of Tiamoon?"

Gitty looked into the smirked face of Morgan. "Get real. That midget of a sister has as much chance of defeating me as you do of convincing the local tavern wenches you're wealthy without using magic."

She watched the sneer on his face morph into a scowl. *Point for me.*

She magicked a hundred dollar bill that she handed to Morgan. "Go play with your little friends but keep your inner ears open. I may call on you. Don't ignore me or you'll live to regret it."

He raised an eyebrow in question, gave Gitty a nod of the head then bolted to his room to shower and get ready for an evening out.

"It's very strange how much magic is pooling around the Lending Library. The air is rippling with waves of enchantments. There is something going on and I need to know what it is. How…?"

Lancelot tread lightly across the floor and undulated around Gitty's legs. She started to scold him and stopped herself. Scooping up the large creature in one hand, she moved to the window at the front of the living room.

"Lancelot, my love," she cooed.

A rumbled purr was her answer. The cat had blanked its mind of all thought.

"Now, now, lovey. I want you to do a task for me. Capture one of the messenger mice."

The mind picture the cat projected was of a mutilated mouse disappearing down his throat.

"No, my love, not for eating."

Lancelot huffed his unhappiness.

"I need information from the creature. Once I have what I need, I don't care what you do with it as long as you don't do it in my house."

"Rrrrooowwww."

Gitty watched the magic dwindle around the Library to small sparkles of light.

"I *will* find out what's happening, Tia. Then you'll regret leaving your safe, comfortable exile."

Chapter Fourteen

Linda slid quietly from her room to a chair she'd set against the back wall. Since the arrival of the small warrior and return of Ailidh and Kayne, life in the Lending Library had been anything but sedate. There were daily arrivals of faeries, wood nymphs, gnomes, sprites, and more wood creatures than she knew existed in this region.

On top of the daily arrivals, the sweet, shy, timid Ailidh who had left clinging to Kayne's arm had returned brandishing an attitude that rivaled the warrior gnome's own brashness. They had taken up sword practice behind the library and the clanging of metal against metal had become routine background noise. Kayne wandered around the first day or two looking lost but soon realized if he were to keep his ladylove, he'd just have to accept the change. Within a short period, he was offering his services as sparing partner for the two female warriors so one or the other of them could rest between practice sessions.

Linda realized her home, her library, had the feel of a base camp of operations during war. The thought frightened her a bit, but she wouldn't turn away any of the fae community. She was now, and always had been, a guest in their world.

The front door opened and several fae men wearing the trappings of clan chiefs entered the premises jostling for lead position.

"Innkeep!" The tallest fae thumped his sword on the wooden floor. "Innkeep! I need a room, a pint, and a willing wench!"

Raucous laughter rolled through the room.

Linda watched Chrissy dart from the kitchen to the front door, her wings a blur of movement.

"Behave yourself, you uncouth, loudmouthed, brute of a creature or I'll throw you out." The little wood nymph plunked herself in front of the two foot tall fae outfitted in chainmail and fawn leather shirt and leggings. His unruly flowing black hair fell loosely down his back. He placed his sword into the scabbard and faced the nymph.

Chrissy straightened to her full height, fisted her hands on her waist, and glared at the interloper, her violet eyes sparking wildly at the warrior.

Linda rose from her spot against the wall not sure how quickly she could cover the distance between her chair and the front door, but determined nothing would harm her friend. She edged along the bookshelves until she noted the sparkle in the deep brown weathered eyes of the fae chieftan.

"Will you now, Crystal of the Glen?"

Chrissy was trying hard but losing the battle to maintain her frightful frown. She giggled then hurled herself into the arms of the faerie.

"Oh, Raghnall! Where have you been? I've missed you so much." She pulled the warrior's face to hers and locked him in a tender kiss that pulled a low moan from deep in his throat.

Breaking the kiss, he sighed and offered a tender, sweet smile to the little nymph.

"When the treaty was signed all those years ago, Tiamoon was not the only one to be exiled. I had to put my mark on the paper and promise never to return to the valley if I wanted my family and," he ran his forefinger down her velvety cheek, "my love to remain healthy and alive. I've missed you so much, my sweet."

Ignoring the pandemonium that was quickly becoming the norm for the Lending Library, the two lovers gazed into each other's eyes. Linda eased her way back to her chair and felt the ache of loss as the sight of the two reunited lovers tugged thoughts of her husband from the recesses of her memory.

I do miss him so.

"What is all the turmoil I'm hearing? Someone is destroying the ancients?" Raghnall nodded at the troupe of men around him. "Rest. We'll camp in the meadow beyond the house tonight. I have business."

A few of the men snickered.

Raghnall turned an icy glare their direction. The sniggering stopped. As the clan chiefs fanned out around the room, he grasped Chrissy's hand and led her to a table.

"I have to get back to the kitchen."

"You what?"

"I work here, Raghnall."

"Why? You're faefolk. We don't need to work."

The corners of Chrissy's mouth tipped up. "I know but I needed something to keep me busy. Most of the other nymphs left after the war and the faeries tend to stick together." She looked at him, water pooling in her eyes, threatening to spill down her cheeks. "I had no one and when they destroyed my tree... well, the Librarian kindly offered the oak behind her house to me. She can see us, Raghnall."

"Who is this Librarian? And what difference does it make if she can see us? I can see you."

"She's an Other?"

His eyes widened. "She's an Other?" He rose hurriedly from his chair knocking it over in his haste. He started toward the door. "I need to get out of here. I don't want anything to do with Others. The night elves..."

"AHA! That proves it!" Chrissy smacked the tabletop.

The noise in the room abated for a moment as all eyes centered on the furious wood nymph.

"It has been the Saun family and night elves all along! This is the first I've heard of you being exiled. Why did you feel you couldn't trust me with the knowledge of their treachery?"

Raghnall swung around, pulling his shoulders back and raising his head high.

"Because it was my choice and my burden to bear. I made the sacrifice for my family, friends, and the woman I love."

Chrissy narrowed her eyes at him. "You were the only family I had,

Raghnall. Mine was all killed in the war. Remember?"

He opened his mouth to respond but was drowned out by the shouts of the other fae warriors.

"Food! Where does a man get some food around here?"

Chrissy looked at him. "We'll continue this discussion later. I have to work now."

She bustled over to a table of rowdy warriors and, dodging grasping hands and leering grins, took their orders.

Raghnall exited to the front porch. He stood, reconnoitering the surrounding meadow and woods. There was a sense of unease in the air that set his nerves to twitching. He felt certain someone was watching. *But who?*

~ * ~

Linda observed the increasing bustle in her home. There were fae of all sizes and shapes. She didn't know why but the realization the fae were as different in form as humans took her by surprise. Then she felt guilty she had presupposed what appearance faeries would take.

"Guess prejudice comes in all forms." She muttered more to herself than anyone else.

The cacophony took on a pattern and Linda sensed liaisons were being formed throughout the room. The conversation around the tables appeared serious in nature. When the speaking ceased, each clan representative would look to the others sharing the table and, with a nod of the head, end the meeting. There would be back slapping and hand shaking then the appearance of little flasks let Linda know the faeries were magicking while she was present.

It was an honor she had never expected to happen. As the day wore on the seriousness of the meetings abated and soon the fae were relating tales of their time away. The atmosphere lost the seriousness of the morning and a relaxing joviality expanded around the room.

Linda noted Chrissy wander to the front porch where she siddled up to Raghnall. He slipped an arm around her waist and the two engaged in quiet conversation. Chrissy's face glowed as she looked up at the faerie warrior and Linda, feeling ever the voyeur, found herself wishing for one more time of feeling the same way. She got up and slipped into the kitchen to clean so Chrissy could spend time with her beau only to find the counters and workspaces spotless.

"You could've asked my help, my little friend…"

Turning on her heel, Linda stopped at the doorway then tiptoed back to her room. She was tired of sitting quietly away from the action. The need to feel fresh air on her face overwhelmed her. Slipping on her tennis shoes, Linda exited through a back door she seldom used anymore. She stood on her small back porch taking in the view of the valley. It had been many months since she gazed at the meadow and surrounding peaks. The mountains still rose majestically from the basin floor and groves of evergreens blanketed their sides. But all was not right with the valley. There was something… missing. Linda squinted at the expanse, narrowing her eyes to focus on the vast terrain in front of her. In the distance among all the green grass of the meadow and surrounding trees, sat a brilliant yellow machine. She started looking at the stands of trees more carefully and realized the oaks were missing in large numbers.

The recognition of this truth chilled her to the bone. If she had not stopped the dozers, they would soon have demolished every stand of oaks in the valley. *But why? What is so important about the oak tress?*

Linda strolled the back of her property until dusk darkened her path. She watched in amazement as the air around her home wavered wildly. *Must be more tired than I thought.* With each step toward her domicile, Linda's tiredness abated. When she stepped on the back porch, she experienced a lightness in her step she'd been missing lately.

The room hummed with activity and laughter smattered around the area. No one noticed her enter nor did her presence interrupt conversation.

They must be getting used to me. She smiled and nodded at a couple fae chieftains who acknowledged her. She changed her sneakers and moved from her bedroom to the kitchen intent on fixing herself a snack when the metallic ringing of multiple swords being drawn stopped her. She snapped around to face the front door and sucked in a deep breath at the sight she beheld.

Looming in the doorway, a figure attired in a floor length, tan duster ducked under the doorframe standing erect once he entered. Short white hair, tanned skin, and eyes so blue they stood out across the room completed the image standing on her landing.

"If he stays, we go!" A warrior attired in all red stood, his sword pointed toward the figure at the door.

"Aye! We'll not stay in the same building as he!" Several others chimed brandishing swords and knocking over chairs in their haste to rise.

Raghnall stepped from behind the tall stranger and lifted his sword. "This man was invited."

"Who would be foolish enough to invite a night elf to our gathering?"

The group muttered their agreement.

"I would."

All eyes turned to Chrissy.

Macartan, a river fae, walked to the nymph and hissed in her face. "And why would you do something so stupid?"

Raghnall sped to Chrissy's side. She looked at him and shook her head.

"Because this is a problem faced by all of us… including the night elves."

Macartan puckered his mouth to spit then thought better of it. He stomped to his table and began gathering his belongings. Many in the room followed suit.

Linda watched as the handsome, extremely tall, stranger stepped toward the center of the room.

"If I may…"

She felt her heart race and unconsciously ran a hand through her hair.

The stranger put up a hand. "I know all of you feel we night elves were the cause of the last war between our races…"

The gathered crowd in the room bellowed agreement.

"…but I'm here to tell you the fighting was initiated and continued by the clan Saun. By the time the rest of our world heard of the war, the Saun's had secured the lands using rogue elves as soldiers and secured treaties signed by many of your clansmen. The use of brute force on another race is forbidden by elvan law. It's not our way."

"Tell that to my dead uncle!"

Chrissy faced the sea of angry warriors. "We *all* experienced loss from the war. It scarred every family represented in this room. I don't think anyone wants to experience the pain of loss again. That's why I asked Uther to join us. Maybe he can help find a solution to our problem that won't involve fighting."

Raghnall stepped next to her. "We have nothing to lose and Uther has taken the fae oath of silence. If he breaks that silence the penalty is…"

"DEATH!" The room roared.

Uther tipped his head in agreement. "Death. Frankly, I have many years left to live in my life. I don't wish to end it too soon."

Macartan dropped his belongings on the floor. "Then you will agree to anything we decide?"

Uther shook his head. "No."

Swords rattled and warriors snarled.

"I won't agree to anything that will end in the loss of life. I do think, however, I may have a solution to benefit us all."

Chrissy cast Raghnall a sideways look.

"If I might request a chair and something to drink? It has been a long journey this day."

Chrissy winged her way to Linda who stood in the doorway of the kitchen gazing Uther's direction. The little nymph smirked at Linda. "Is he not the most beautiful man you have ever seen?"

Linda felt heat flame her cheeks. "I, uh, guess so."

"Would you help me get him a chair and some water?"

"Of course. How rude I am."

Chrissy giggled. "Uther has that effect on people."

Linda dragged the chair she normally used toward the front door. As she neared the night elf, her senses began to work overtime. She licked her lips and cursed the moisture forming in her palms. Her mouth felt dry and she knew she must look a sight. *Why didn't I run a comb through my hair after my walk?* She sighed in resignation.

A pitcher of water and a glass had been set on a table near the elf. Linda brought the chair and set it on the floor. As she was about to make her escape, a gentle hand on her arm stopped her. She turned to see who was holding up her progress from fleeing the room and long forgotten sensations.

"Thank you." Uther's deep silky voice vibrated the air around him.

"You're… you're welcome." She knew her cheeks were blazing red and she moved her gaze to the floor.

Chrissy flitted over to the table. "Uther? This is the Other I was telling you about. She's opened her home to us, given me a place to live, and agreed to help if there is anything she might do. This is Linda."

"Pleased to meet you Linda. I find it fascinating there is an Other who believes in our existence."

Linda squirmed. "My family is from Ireland, and I grew up with the tales of faeries and elves. I'm just luckier than most; I can see everyone."

An unseen force drew her gaze to the eyes she'd noted from the other side of the building. She looked into the cool blue orbs and found herself ensnared in their kindness. The hand resting on her arm halting her attempt to flee was strong. Well-formed fingers with calluses showing a practiced work ethic detained her escape but didn't clutch her in force.

"Your name is spoken throughout the magic community with respect. There are some in my clan who could afford to take a lesson from your actions."

Her lips moved but no sound emerged. Her cheeks flared hotly.

He smiled; a slow enveloping movement that lit the room with brilliance. His hand dropped from her arm to his side.

"You give no thought to personal gain. That's unusual in both our worlds. I hope to learn much from you during this meeting of clans."

Linda cleared her throat. "I believe it is I who has much to learn. I hope I'm worthy of the privilege."

Chrissy smiled and winked at Uther. "I think so, Librarian, but then I know you."

Linda quickly escaped to the back of the library and disappeared into her room.

~ * ~

Uther gazed at the wood nymph. "Do you really believe she is worthy of standing for the Others in this meeting?"

Chrissy snapped around and stared at the night elf.

He watched her tiny body shake with anger, her wings rustling with the effort she was making not to explode into a tirade.

"I had to ask. Your reaction tells me what I need to know."

"Ahhh!" Chrissy streaked to the kitchen, the sounds of metal against metal letting all know of her anger.

Uther turned to look at Raghnall who'd been standing quietly back and observing the conversation. "She's quite outspoken, is she not?"

Raghnall shook his head. "You have no idea *how* outspoken. Had the Others' women not taken up the cause of equality first; our own would have demanded such rights a long time ago."

Uther flashed a wide grin. "Ah, but it puts spice in to life."

Dragging sounds of metal on wood interrupted the conversation. Tiamoon pushed through a throng of fae warriors congregating at the door.

"Where is he? I heard he actually had the nerve to show his face in these woods. Where is that devil Uther?"

She swung around to find herself facing the very soul she sought.

"Uther!"

"Tiamoon."

"So have you come back to try and finish what your kind started all those years ago? We're better armed now, and many of us have been practicing for just this occasion."

"No, my fierce little warrior. I came to clear up some myths about the night elves in the last war and to make sure there is no war this time."

Tia narrowed her eyes at the creature whose kind had forsaken her to live near her family and friends. "Do *not* make assumptions based upon the size of a thing, elf. The sharpness of my blade doesn't judge the size of the thing it cuts."

Raghnall stepped between the two. "Tia, Uther. Let's not start on bitter ground. It's time for the clans to sit, discuss, and decide how we will handle the problem we all face. Uther says he may have a solution. Let's hear him out before we throw him out. What do you say, Tia?"

The gnome glowered at the elf. A barely perceptible nod signaled the beginning of the first meeting of the clans in nearly 80 years. Raghnall stepped outside to the porch and pulling a horn from his side, blew three short blasts. An hour later, the fae warrior called the meeting to order.

~ * ~

Linda peeked out at the roomful of clan chieftains and warriors of all sizes. The gleam of silver blades in the light set goose bumps on her skin.

Several of the higher clan chiefs spoke and were well received. Points were made about what was happening in the valley; homes being damaged, innocents nearly being killed, and Ancients being completely destroyed. The atmosphere was heading toward heated when the night elf stood and cleared his throat.

"I've heard enough to know what I'm about to propose is the best solution to rid this valley of the threat… permanently."

Chapter Fifteen

Gitty pulled the barbell up for one more curl before dropping it on the stand. She grabbed the nearby towel and wiped the sweat from her forehead. *I'm done.*

She'd found herself in the basement gym more often these last few weeks since the construction company had been closed down. *Temporarily, only temporarily.* She headed for the shower. Letting the hot liquid sluice down her pumped muscles, Gitty relaxed until the water ran lukewarm. A change of clothing and the growling of her stomach demanded an immediate response.

As she stood waiting for the microwave to finish heating her meal, Lancelot trotted across the flagstone floor.

"Where've you been, you mangy beast? I thought I told you to grab one of the messenger mice so we could find out what's going on in the valley. Well? What happened?"

Lancelot turned his back to her as he drank from his water bowl. Gitty, unable to see into his mind unless she looked directly in his eyes, walked over and picked up the cat. She held him in her arms and stared into his golden orbs. Once connection had been made she got the pictures she was seeking.

"What? No mice *anywhere*?" She unceremoniously dropped the cat to the floor. "Vermin infested monsters are in hiding. I can sense something big is happening, and I aim to find out what. Better to be one step ahead than one step behind."

The microwave dinged in response and Gitty retrieved her food.

She sat at the kitchen table, microwave food container on a heating pad, fork held mid-air, staring morosely out at the woods below. She could see the glow of lights from the Lending Library and all day long she'd been feeling the light fingers of magic dancing across her arms. The warmth of the room and heat from food in her belly began to lull Gitty's eyelids downward. The muscles of her neck relaxed and her shoulders slumped. *A quick nap would feel so good.*

Leather boots thudding on the stone flooring interrupted the pleasant moment. The harsh sound drew closer, preceded by a wave of unpleasantness dispelling the magic's warmth. Gitty pushed her food away and looked up at the sour expression on the face of her brother as he stomped into the kitchen area.

"What's the matter, Morgan? Won't anyone come out and play with you?"

He growled at her. "What would you know about playing? No one can stand to be near you."

"My but we're touchy this evening. Did some gnome steal your best girl?"

Morgan strode to the window and peered toward the valley, arms clasped behind his back.

Gitty began to worry. Morgan never let a chance go by to try and outdo her insults. His silence was unnerving.

"Morgan? What happened out there tonight? You're home entirely too early."

Gitty watched the broad back of her brother rise and fall with a deep sigh.

"We have a *very* large problem, Gitty."

She rolled her eyes. "For elves sake, Morgan, don't go drama king on me. What in the name of dragons and unicorns are you talking about?"

The tall night elf dropped his hands to his side and shook his head. He turned to face his sister.

"I hit a couple of my local haunts to see if any of my favorites were out with no luck. It was pretty quiet so I made my way north. There are a

couple clubs near the university I've avoided because young Others are so-
-so…"

"Human?" Gitty raised an eyebrow.

Morgan narrowed his eyes and pushed out an exasperated sigh. "No. So unbelieving. The younger women still believe they're attractive to any and all men. They're harder to convince than the older ones who've had their hearts broken. Anyway, I strolled into several clubs and found myself welcomed for about an hour until the young girls got tired of buying my drinks.

"They informed me I wasn't anything like the 'other tall, white-haired guy with really cool icy blue eyes'."

"Like this is news?" She held her chin in the palm of her hand, her elbow resting on the tabletop. "So?"

Morgan glared at his sister.

"I decided to push a little and see who this guy was. I asked around to see if anyone could remember his name. A couple of the girls giggled and nodded their heads. They said he had an unusual name; something really medieval, like Geoffrey or Arthur or something like that."

"Morgan? Is there a point to all of this rambling?"

"Gitty!"

"What?!"

"Quit being such an ass."

Gitty dropped her hand to the table and raised her eyebrows at her brother. "What did you call me?"

Morgan puffed out his cheeks in frustration. "Think! What tall, white-haired guy with blue eyes and a medieval name do we know?"

Gitty stood, the chair scraping the floor. "I'm done. This is a guessing game for children, and I haven't been a child in over 100 years. Why don't you go online and tell your tall tales to some of your Internet lovers? You can still magic over distances, can't you?"

She trudged from the kitchen toward the hallway and her bedroom.

"Uther."

The name, spoken softly, stopped all movement in the household;

even Lancelot stopped eating, flattened his ears against his head, and growled.

Gitty stopped in the middle of the hallway and turned. Her face had drained of all color and her eyes were the size of the tea saucers in the cupboard.

"What did you say?" She whispered.

"Uther."

She walked back to the living room and fell on to the couch. "It--it just can't be."

"Why not? Because he fears the Sauns and the house of Saun? I doubt it."

"No, because I was sure I'd seen our father put a blade to him. He was sprawled on the ground; blood everywhere, not breathing. I was certain of it!"

Morgan moved to the wingback chair and lowered himself into the plush upholstery.

"Well, sister dear, apparently you were wrong. There is an elvan man in these parts calling himself Uther and being kind to everything and everyone.

"If he is the same Uther… we're in trouble." Morgan turned to his sister. "We need to find out what's happening in that library place before it gets out of hand and we lose everything."

Gitty snapped her head his direction. "You *think*? I've been trying to get you to see what's been going on for the last month, but you've been too busy leeching off your girlfriends to see beyond your next free drink.

"Closing down our company was just the beginning," Gitty got up from the couch and paced back and forth. "The longer we're closed, the more chance there is someone will find the treasure Thomas talked about. If he told me in a drunken stupor, you can be sure he told someone else too."

She shuddered, stopping to cross her arms over her chest.

"I can't swear to it but it feels as if the magic level of the surrounding area has risen one hundred fold. I continually feel the buzzing of cast spells. Before, when it was just the two of us, the air was still until we used our own magic. Now, there's constant movement. The key to all of this lies inside the Lending Library."

The siblings turned and stared at the small rooftop. Light shown from the windows and the meadow moved with activity.

Gitty nodded her head. "I think it's time to make a neighborly visit."

Morgan frowned at his sister. "Why would we want to do that? You don't read."

She huffed out a breath, rolled her eyes, and shook her head. "You are such an idiot."

"What?"

"Think. What is the best way to find out what is happening?"

"I don't know."

Gitty dropped her head and let her hands drop to her side. Looking up at her sibling with eyes blazing, she gritted her teeth as she answered.

"How have you lived so long without being killed? The best way to find out what is happening is to *be* there when it happens. If we make a friendly visit to the Library, should Tiamoon or some of her pathetic little friends show up, we'd know about it because…"

"…we'd be there." Morgan brightened as he finished his sister's sentence.

"Uhhgg." Gitty shook her had and headed down the hallway. "I'm going to bed."

Morgan turned his attention to the light in the valley. "Maybe there'll be some women who don't know me there." The reflection in the window showed a lecherous smile spreading over his face.

Chapter Sixteen

Tiamoon sat in the child-sized chair and propped her legs, crossed at the ankle, on the lower slat of the porch railing. She made a visual reconnoiter of the surrounding area. There were a few spots of wavering air consistent with magic being used, but beyond that nothing was happening. The calmness made her uncomfortable. With her step-siblings so close, she didn't trust the serenity. She sensed the presence before noting his fawn colored boots standing next to her.

"Tiamoon."

"Uther."

"May I join you?"

"Still a free country."

The elf sat on the top step his long legs stretched languidly in front of him.

"Do you sense Gitty and Morgan nearby?"

Tia shifted her weight and recrossed her feet. "No. There's nothing here for them to gain. I know elvan magic is stronger than fae magic, one on one, but with so many fae present, the two would have to be out of their minds to attempt any confrontation. I also suspect they've felt your presence. Gitty may be bold, but she's not stupid. Everyone in the fae kingdom knows how powerful you are."

Uther smiled at the compliment. "Thank you, I think. I'm powerful but no more than any other night elf. I've just learned to utilize what's been given me. Two night elves in tandem against me could easily defeat me. I hope circumstances don't take that turn."

Tia snorted. "I can't see Gitty and Morgan *ever* doing anything in tandem. The only reason they live in the same house without killing each other is our father demanded it."

Uther raised an eyebrow and shot the gnome a side look.

"Yeah. We share a father, nothing more. When he was killed in the war, those two sent my mother away and exiled me. They wanted to make sure no one knew we were related. Hence, the stepbrother, stepsister verbage. It was as if anyone knowing we shared the same blood would taint them in your community. I couldn't have cared but it brought an early end to my mother's life. She idolized my father and willingly accepted his children. The feelings were not mutual.

"Anyway, I hope you know what you're doing with this party idea."

Uther leaned himself back on his elbows stretching to his full length. "I've sensed them watching the building."

Tia's eyebrows shot up.

"Yes. They're keeping an eye on the unusual amount of fae traffic in and out of the house. They, too, can feel the spike of magic around the Library. If, as you say, control and power is foremost in their minds, they'll want to make sure they're prepared to protect what they have. Any attempt to overtake them will be met with brutal, deadly force.

"The party tonight will peak their curiosity. I'm surprised they haven't shown before now."

Tiamoon humphed. "Gitty likes to sneak up and ambush people. Walking up to the front door and knocking is not her style."

The two warriors sat quietly for a moment soaking in the smells and sights of a spring day in the forest. Sun filtered between the trees exposing new life on the forest floor. A gentle breeze wafted the sweet scent of early flowers celebrating the break from the constant rain and cold of winter.

"Has anyone figured out why the Sauns are killing the Ancients?" Uther sat up, placed his elbows on his knees, and stared down the driveway.

"No. That's the strangest thing of all. About ten to eleven months ago, seemingly out of the blue, they started tearing up the oak groves; nothing else, just oaks. The construction equipment appeared and a sign went up announcing a new subdivision of houses according to the Librarian. However, nothing was built, just the destruction of the oaks."

"Then our mission is twofold; stop the Sauns wanton destruction of the Ancients and finding out *why* they're killing the forest."

~ * ~

Ailidh and Kayne slowed their trek as they neared home. The tree still stood and she turned to him, a smile touching her lips.

"We may still have a place to live!"

Kayne looked around the meadow. He felt exposed and vulnerable walking in the open.

"Ailidh? Let's just check out the tree and get back to the library. Something is not right about this place."

"Oh, don't be silly." Ailidh pushed open the door. Dust covered every item in the living area, but nothing had been taken or moved. It was as they had left it nearly two months earlier. She pushed a sigh through her lips, her shoulders relaxing, and smiled widely.

"We're home, Kayne. We're home."

Kayne had been backing into the trunk of the oak that served as home to the fae pair, watching the horizon for trouble. His magic sense tingled with danger warnings. He'd turned, gripped the door, and was pushing it closed when a large black paw clutched the side and shoved.

"Ailidh! Run!"

Enormous gold eyes gleamed dangerously as the cat tried to push its way into the hole. It swiped the air with one paw, pushing the door inward with the other.

Kayne tried to push back but the creature's size and weight made the battle an uneven match.

"Kayne! The incantation!" Ailidh drew her sword, closed her eyes, and pointed toward the door. She began chanting.

"I command you, I compel you, creature of Gitty, get out of my house now!"

Kayne added his voice raising it until he was shouting at the black intruder.

Chanting the incantation, Ailidh opened her eyes, glared at the enormous yellow-eyed monster, and pushed toward the door. A high-pitched keening began to rent the air. The cat dug its heels in pushing backwards from the tree and, yeowling in pain, fled. The two faeries watched the monster streak from their home in the oak.

Ailidh looked at Kayne a smug smile on her face.

"Welcome home."

~ * ~

Linda watched the activity in her lending library. The building was humming. She couldn't believe how many of the small magical folk were inside the walls of her home. Childhood dreams never included this many faeries in one place. The hub of activity was Chrissy's kitchen. The little wood nymph had taken control of the celebration planning and was barking out orders like a general planning a campaign.

"No, Rory, not there; near the doorway."

"What difference does it make? They're not gonna notice it anyway."

"No, but I am."

Throwing up his hands, the warrior-turned-unwilling-room-decorator moved the floral display.

"Women!"

Linda couldn't stop the giggle that escaped her. Chrissy was a force to be reckoned with.

She'd been so busy watching the decorating, she'd not taken notice of where she was walking. Bumping into a muscular, wide chest, Linda felt the heat flood her cheeks. She immediately looked to the ground and apologized.

"I'm so sorry. My mistake."

A hand gently cupped her chin and brought her head up. She found herself looking directly into the stunning blue eyes of the night elf Uther. Again, her cheeks flooded with heat.

"Please don't apologize to me. The fae folk are notorious for not trusting anything they haven't invented or been around in the last 200 years. Frankly, I think they owe you a debt of gratitude for offering your home as a refuge."

"I agree." Chrissy interjected as she sped past her wings churning furiously. "Laughlin! Not there! *Why* didn't they bring their mates? Aaahhhh!"

Uther chuckled.

Linda felt the sound roll over her skin and tickle her ears. This beautiful man was reminding her of sensations she'd long put away. It made her uncomfortable on the one hand and happy on the other that she could still feel.

"I'm happy to have my house full of life again."

Uther smiled. "Yes, Chrissy told me of your brave fight to help your husband in his last days. He was a lucky man."

"I miss him." Linda looked horrified she had confided something so personal to a virtual stranger. "I'm sorry. That was very… rude. If you'll excuse me?"

She fled out to her backyard. Tiamoon was practicing her sword moves alone. Linda slipped past the gnome warrior and walked the fence line to the back of the property. A small creek served as the demarcation of the end of her property. Linda found her favorite stump and sat staring at the rippling water.

"Are you okay?"

She jumped at the sound of the deep voice.

"No. I'm flustered, confused, overwhelmed… you name it. I had my life all planned out then my husband got sick and died. So--I changed my plans. I indulged my love of books and surrounded myself with items I knew wouldn't die or require me to do more than love them.

"Then Chrissy showed up. I couldn't believe all the tales my relatives told me were true and standing in front of me in the form of a wood nymph. I guess I got carried away thinking they would ever accept me.

"Then you showed up..."

Uther nodded. "And I stirred feelings you thought long dead."

Linda's mouth dropped. She put a hand over it and nodded her agreement.

He smiled. "No ,I don't read minds but you *are* fairly see-through. You don't hide your feelings very well."

She shrugged. "Yeah, Donald always did say I was an open book."

Uther knelt to the side of the stump and gently placed Linda's hand in his.

"If I may say... you are still a magnificent looking woman, Librarian..."

"Linda."

He tipped his head. "Linda. I would be honored if you would allow me to become a friend."

She turned her head and peered into his face. "I'd like that."

A grin touched his lips. "We can see where it goes from there."

Linda blushed. "Darn this blushing stuff."

Uther chuckled. "I find it attractive and honest. Would you like me to leave you to your thoughts?"

"Maybe for a little bit. Chrissy has everything so under control I feel in the way in my own home. I sure hope this works out for everyone."

Uther stood, kissed the hand he held and placed it in her lap. "So do I."

~ * ~

Gitty walked the perimeter of her property noting the increasing activity at the Lending Library. She felt a pressing, unrelenting need to be there; so much so the need wretched her senses to the point of restlessness. Uther was there--she could *feel* his presence. *Before this night is over, Uther, there will be a shift in power in this valley.*

Gitty strode to the house and, upon entering, called for her brother.

"Morgan! It's time we met our neighborhood librarian. Get down here!"

She heard the laconic shuffle of feet and looked up to see Morgan dressed in a running suit and shoes ambling his way toward her.

"Oh, no, little brother. Get back upstairs and put on your best dress-to-impress outfit. For the most part you're useless, but unsettling the ladies with your first impression is what I need to give us the advantage. Move it!"

Morgan stuck out his lower lip and pouted as he turned around and trudged back to his room to change.

When he returned and received Gitty's approval, the pair climbed into the Hummer and drove to the Lending Library. The closer they got to the building the more agitated Gitty felt.

"There is a lot of magic being performed in this vicinity." She parked the car out front and exited her side. Morgan followed suit, allowing Gitty to take the lead. She walked up the steps of the quaint building and read the sign on the door--Open. Just walk in.

~ * ~

Uther shushed the noisy crowd as he watched the night elf pair ascend the steps.

"They're here. Shhhh!"

~ * ~

She pushed the door open slowly, unsure of what she would find on the other side. Once in the building there was a festive atmosphere, floral arrangements adorned walls and the tables had tablecloths and centerpieces. An older woman in a stunning blue dress came from the back room and jumped when she saw the pair.

"Oh! I'm sorry. You startled me. Welcome to the Lending Library.

We're celebrating our 10th anniversary with a party. You're welcome to stay if you like."

Her smile was bright and Gitty returned the gesture.

"Hello. I'm Gitty Saun and this is my brother Morgan." She turned around and grabbed him by the coat muttering under her breath. "Get over here, you idiot."

From behind the tall, white-haired woman's back, stepped a man with waist-length white hair and deep blue eyes. Linda sucked in a breath, smiling to cover her surprise. Uther had warned her Morgan was handsome, but his warning paled in comparison to the reality. The man smiled, showing a set of dazzling white teeth, but Linda noted the smile didn't reach his eyes.

"Pleased to meet you."

Linda subtly stepped back and slightly to the side. "I'm Linda and this is…"

"UTHER!"

The brother and sister spoke in unison. Their faces were locked in an expression of shock when Uther pulled his staff and pointed it their direction.

"FREEZE!"

The two forms were trapped in the positions they had been standing when the night elf had cast a stunning spell on them. Linda watched as their eyes blinked.

Uther lifted each of the night elves separately and carried them to the center of the room standing them side-by-side. Once in place, the room filled with fae warriors, wood nymphs, gnomes, and forest creatures.

Tiamoon walked from the back porch to face the elvan pair.

"Gitty and Morgan Saun."

Linda swore she could see hatred radiate from the pair's eyes.

"You have terrorized this valley for many decades; killing many of our relatives, stealing from those who remained, and banishing others as you saw fit. Your actions have indicted you. The fae clans, along with Uther representing the Night Elves and the Librarian representing the Others, have decreed that as long as you wish to act like the humans, you will live like the humans and die like the humans."

Tiamoon nodded and the elvan pair watched as clan chieftans came from various parts of the room and stood in front of them. Uther and the person they called the Librarian moved to the back of the fae. The group looked directly into the eyes of the two rogue night elves while Tiamoon spoke.

"Guardians of magic, your hearts have strayed,
You seek wealth and power and have chosen the dark way.
This council has voted to speak as one,
We withhold your powers from this day on.
No longer will you use the Old Magic ways,
A human life you'll live for the rest of your days.
All the room pointed at the elves and spoke in unison.
Gitty and Morgan Saun: It is over, it is done.
Gitty and Morgan Saun: It is over, it is done.
Gitty and Morgan Saun: It is over, it is done."

Uther moved to face the elves and lifted his staff pointing it their direction.

"FREE!"

The startled expression on the two faces turned to frowning snarls, and the two began to flex muscles and move around.

"Don't think this is over, you little freaks. You've just made the biggest enemy you could have in your lifetimes." Gitty lifted a hand toward Tiamoon. "Destroy!"

Silence filled the room.

Tiamoon stood tall, her right hand clutching the handle of her sword. She looked at the woman who'd exiled her and smiled.

"Like to try that again?"

"MORGAN! Help me!"

The two elves stood pointing at the gnome and yelled together. "Destroy!"

A ripple of laughter passed through the room when nothing

happened.

Gitty's face blossomed to a bright red. "AAAAHHHHH! I still have the construction company and I'll bulldoze every stand of trees in this valley!"

"I don't think so." Uther moved to face Gitty.

She glared at him, her fists clenching and unclenching. "Oh? Do you really think I care what you think? My crews will make matchsticks of this building then I'll dig until I find the blasted treasure that drunken leprechaun babbled on about."

Linda stepped forward. "Treasure? There's a treasure in my house?"

Morgan had slinked to the door and attempted to leave. Several fae chieftans held him at sword point inside the room as Tiamoon walked up to face him.

"You're not going anywhere, brother dearest."

She watched him flinch at her use of the word brother.

Gitty narrowed her eyes and spit her words out through clenched teeth. "Yes, treasure, as if you didn't know."

Linda looked at her. "What leprechaun?"

Gitty rolled her eyes. "Others. You're all so stupid."

Uther moved toward Gitty. "Watch your mouth."

"Or you'll do what?"

Linda stood, finger tapping on her chin. She looked at Uther and a smile spread to cover her whole face. "Is he a short man with an Irish accent and bright green eyes?"

Gitty shook her head. "That describes three quarters of the men in this valley."

"A little man who speaks of enough gold bricks to build a mansion?"

Gitty stopped and turned to Linda. "That's the one."

Linda bit her lip to keep from laughing but gave into the urge. Soon she was holding her sides and guffawing.

The effect soon had the room responding the same way.

"WHAT IS SO DAMN FUNNY?"

Linda stopped laughing long enough to look directly into the eyes of the angry female night elf.

"Thomas always told me my books were worth more than any monetary fortune. In fact, he made up a little ditty just for me.

A stand of oaks
That all can see,
Hides the fortune
Most seek from me.

Linda watched the vein in the elf's neck throb. Her face turned purple and she screamed as she ran from the room grabbing her brother in her escape. Linda looked at Uther.

"She's quite upset. Are my forest folk really safe from them?"

He nodded. "Yes. They've lost their magic. Right now, they don't understand what that means, but next time they try to magic something away, nothing will happen. They wanted the power and life of humans, now they have it until they die."

Linda shook her head. "How sad. For something as fleeting as power, they gave up the most important thing of all--they sold their heritage."

Uther slipped her hand into his. "It's their loss. Now, let's not worry about them and celebrate. This week has resulted in a gathering of clans that hasn't been seen in many decades. The valley now has its rightful owners back, and I have a new friend I intend to visit often.

"Is there any cake?"

Linda felt her cheeks flush. "I believe I can arrange that."

The Lending Library
is featured in
A Valentine's Anthology

The Lending Library-a fantasy by C. L. Kraemer

Faeries try to fit into the human world when the forest where they make their home is destroyed by a mysterious enemy.

Chasing Rainbows-a contemporary romance by Genene Valleau
An eccentric aunt, an inventive uncle, a mother who wears poodle skirts, and a brother who wears pearls provide a hilarious backdrop for the courtship of a young woman who yearns for a "normal" family.

The Gift-an historical romance by Christine Young
A man and a woman on opposite sides of the Civil War get a second chance at love after one final battle returns soldiers to their war-torn homes to rebuild their lives.

Available at Rogue Phoenix Press
www.roguephoenixpress.com

Other books by Christie L. Kraemer
Available at Rogue Phoenix Press

Healthy Homicide

Two murders have occurred at the Barrel Springs Day Spa. Police hurry to find the method and reason before anyone else is murdered.

MANIC READER REVIEWS says: Healthy Homicide by C.L. Kraemer is an intriguing plot driven mystery. The plot is well written and pretty much carries the whole story...

Dragons Among Us

In a world full of anomalies such as the platypus and self reproducing Komodo dragon, is the human race willing to accept that dragons may be real?

Sapien Draconi-human-dragon shape shifters-all over the world face this dilemma every day. The question has become life and death as their species is plagued with unexpected and unwanted shifting in the most unlikely of places.

The Ancient Ones-full-blooded dragons-can offer advice, but few seem to put forward workable solutions to the problem.

The fate of the shape shifters hangs in the balance, and an answer must be found before the Homo Sapiens find, dissect, and hunt Sapien Draconi to extinction.

Dragons Among the Eagles

Aleda Sable faces the toughest decision of her life--to stay in dragon form, live as a two-legged or put one foot in the human world and one talon in the dragon world.

An urgent call from her newspaper editor sends Aleda to report on an accident whose driver appears to be a dragon. Authorities have the scene locked down and aren't allowing access to anyone. Television broadcasts flash pictures of scaly legs hanging from a crashed car. However, the bodies disappear into thin air. When the stations try follow-up reports, all they find are state highway workers busily tearing up the roads.

In determining the truth of the shifter disappearances, Aleda finds the truth of her own dilemma.

Shattered Tomorrows

Lucy Daniels has a secret--a deeply guarded secret.

Her life was going along just fine until she accompanied her best friend, Cassie, to her attorney's suite on top of the Equitable Building in downtown Salem, Oregon.

Once inside the lawyer's office, the world turned upside down and Lucy was forced to face a demon from her past. Thirty years ago, life had been different. Lucy had discovered Prince Charming and was headed to her happily ever after.

That's when the devil intervened and because of her brush with the devil, innocent people died.

A St. Patrick's Day Tale
by
Christine Young, C. L. Kraemer, Genene Valleau

Tumble through time…

…to Ireland in 1817, when tensions are high between Protestants and Chatolics and faey people guide the fate of villagers. A lovely Catholic lass stumbles upon the weakly ritual fisticuffing between Irish lads. She falls into the lap of a handsome young Protestant. Family ties, grudges, and two conniving faeries threaten their budding love. But the faeries outsmart themselves when they hijack a time machine that has mysteriously appeared in their forest and are whisked to…

…Eugene, Oregon in the 20th century, amid a property feud between the local faeries and night elves. The conniving faeries from Olde Ireland try to stir up more mischief. However, a warrior gnome convinces the magic folk to control their own destiny, and forces the intruding faeries to take refuge in the time machine again, spinning their way toward…

…A modern day castle in western Oregon. An eccentric inventor is determined to reclaim his wayward time machine and save his beloved wife from her latest misadventure. If only they can travel safely past the black hole…

www.ingramcontent.com/pod-product-compliance
Lightning Source LLC
Chambersburg PA
CBHW070635130626
46555CB00006B/2551